JUNE OLDHAM was born and brought up in Lincolnshire. After graduating with a degree in English at Manchester University, she entered teaching but left in order to devote her time to writing, and later to bringing up her two children. Once they were in school she returned to teaching part time in Further Education, and began to write again. Her previous published works have all been in the field of children's and young people's fiction: *A Narrow Escape* (1973), *Wraggle Taggle War* (1977), *The Raven Waits* (1979) and *Enter Tom* (1985). *Grow Up, Cupid* is to be published in 1986.

June Oldham now lives in West Yorkshire. She has been involved with the Ilkley Literature Festival since its inception in 1973, and in 1982 was the festival's director. Since then she has worked in community arts, undertaking a short-term writing residency in Corby, Northamptonshire in 1983, and in 1984 and 1985 had an Arts Council of Great Britain Writing Fellowship in two small communities in Derbyshire.

Flames, June Oldham's first adult novel, is winner of the joint Yorkshire Arts Association and Virago Fiction Prize. Intense and understated, it is a beautifully written work which portrays the tragedy of two lives which, while joined in marriage and parenthood, are separated by unbreachable differences of temperament and upbringing. The consequences spill over into a watching, waiting community; tension builds then snaps, exacting a terrible cost in humiliation and despair. It is a bitter but not inescapable legacy for the next generation.

GW00727852

Flames

June Oldham

VIRAGO

First published by VIRAGO PRESS Limited 1986
41 William IV Street, London WC2N 4DB

Copyright © June Oldham 1986

All rights reserved

British Library Cataloguing in Publication Data
Oldham, June
Flames
I. Title
823'.914 [F]   PR6065.L3/

ISBN 0-86068-739-2
ISBN 0-86068-744-9

Typeset by Goodfellow and Egan and
printed by Anchor Brendon, Tiptree, Essex

Chapter One

'Through that door.' The official looked at them without curiosity as he pointed. The folding places in his white jacket were still pinched in thin ridges by starch. They had not been expected.

'You don't have to come with me,' she said to Michael.

'I'm coming.'

The door had no lettering on it to distinguish it from the rest but it had been left slightly open. For this she was thankful. She pushed the knob and slipped round, followed by her husband; and it was only as she leant back and heard the latch snap home she recalled that at the moment of touching the knob she had tapped questingly on the panel with the knuckles of her other hand.

The sheet sloped down in folds which had neither the symmetry of sculpture nor the chance ruches formed by a natural posture beneath, but were careless, arranged in haste. This she saw and precisely understood, together with the dun crucifix and the arrested wax flowers, as his head, uncovered, commanded her to attend. For even now, frozen and nothing, he was not sufficient. The white starched attendant had set the head to face the door and it inclined, almost lolled towards her, as if in supplication. Waiting for her to come. Sure of his daughter's coming. For a moment she resisted, then she moved to him.

1

As she reached him, something glinted at her out of the slanted face. The body did not move; the face remained fixed, but in the twilight recess formed by the tilted head a white shard bulged. Like a fossil it was held between the open, rigid lids, its plastic an anachronism mocking her out of the dead face; while, bordered with unflecked green, the pupil point squinted. Gasping, she leant forward and plucked at the upper lid and cried out at the prick of the bristle lashes and the repelling ice of the flesh.

'Stella, don't. Leave it. It's too late.'

She ignored him. Supporting herself against the frame of the trolley, she poked at the hollow stud. It swivelled in its setting; the deltas of painted veins flowed under her nails; the iris winked as she prodded and stroked.

'It makes him look as if he could see. As if he could see me.'

'Leave it, Stella, please.' But he did not stretch to restrain her and he watched her fingers do to the other a private violence which strangers had shunned, until at last her nails found an edge and she prised out the opaque shell. Triumphantly she held it up to Michael before looking round quickly like a thief and dropping it among the litter of her bag.

Behind its place the tissues had dried brown. His dark side was quiet now and more seemly. Bending over him, she traced a forefinger along the bow of the socket's lip and, as if concluding a vigil, she smoothed her hand down the closed lid of the other and felt the congealed curve underneath, a pebble stuck in a cranny out of the light. Then she walked back to the door. There she turned and once again regarded him, still in the attitude of tense waiting under his shroud. She averted her head, but she could not leave him in this last condition disappointed and repulsed, so finally surrendering she returned to the bier and leant over his

2

head. Coarse textured, still growing out of the cold stone, his hair gave under the pressure of her mouth and she felt the scalp's frost on her lips.

'You need a drink,' her husband said.

'No.'

'All the same,' he insisted.

The pub was almost empty but it knew its customers and, strangers, they were eyed guardedly. Though he chose a sheltered corner, Michael whispered.

'I was given these. I signed for them. They were on him when he was taken in.'

In the envelope was his watch, small change, a cigarette lighter, a wallet. Michael opened the wallet and showed her three pound notes, several pay slips and a wedding snapshot preserved between two pieces of newspaper. Neither of them lingered over it. The careful memento of their marriage was incongruous among the belongings of the other man and, seeing themselves staring from the glossy card, they shivered as if they were part of his death. Also they felt like spies.

'There isn't much,' she said, pushing everything back into the envelope. 'He was so cold and alone. It seems wrong to leave him there by himself.'

'There is nothing else we can do. I phoned Mrs Livesey and made all the arrangements. Is there anyone else we should contact? Anyone who may wish to attend?'

'I don't think so. If it were taking place in the village, lots of people would go.'

'I suppose so, though I don't think you'd like it. After all, with his reputation there, I imagine that their only reason for attending would be a kind of macabre curiosity.'

'That would be something,' she answered. 'It might be a start.'

Chapter Two

He carried the snapshot of their wedding because afterwards
that was all people wanted to see.

      How's that girl of yours nowadays? workmates would
        ask him.
      Got married a bit back, they would tell a newcomer.
      Here, show him the photo. Don't generally need
        telling,
      But a bit slow today, chum; had a skinful last night.
      What d'you think, then? She's not a bad looker.
      Takes after her dad, old one-eyed Nelson,
      If you look at him sideways.
      Got his brains, too. Or are they her mother's?
      Should have, by all accounts, she's had plenty of
        schooling,
      More than her dad.

So he bore with them, the closer acquaintance a little
fearful though wishing to hearten him, while the younger
ones humoured him dutifully then sniggered together when
he had gone.

    He had never needed prompting to show the photograph
the wedding had displaced. Brown, thumbed and frayed at
the edges, it lay in a drawer under the Three Nuns tobacco
tin in which he kept tie pins and studs. Other men could
grow tired of it and go after something more recent but

there would never be one like that old one, kept safe and flat there under the tin, showing a young girl laughing into the camera he held, saying his name. It was perfect, just as it should be, and without a blur. You could say that snap alone was worth every penny the camera had cost him.

'I'll have a word with Micky, see if I can get one on the club,' he had said to Alice without thinking.

She glanced up from washing the child. 'I wish you wouldn't. I'd rather pay down.' Her preference was as immediate as his.

'You look like our mam sparring for a fight,' he approved. Though you would not come across two women more different.

Her lips thinned with distaste. 'Not me. But there are others besides you would like to see it. Do you know, Mr Thorpe sent a message into school this morning saying I was to thrash his boy if he gave any trouble? Fancy, his father saying that!'

Hubert chuckled. 'Little devil, is he, then?'

'He doesn't like work and fidgets as if he had ants in his pants most of the time, but that's no reason for hitting him. He's only a baby.' She had taught herself to believe there were other ways of behaving, had fabricated in childhood daydreams an ideal which had made the present more temporary and bearable. 'He's only just started school. I wish his father hadn't said that.'

'Better than him turning up and giving it you. I remember our mam grabbing our teacher at the gates and going for her, hammer and tongs. "Don't you ever call my lad names," she was shouting, us kids crouched behind the wall laughing fit to bust and her with her hands full of hair, yanking and puffing, four foot ten and you'd see if she'd swallowed a pickled onion. And she could clout. Send you for six if you wasn't ready. Freer with them than Dad, but

5

once he'd started, Christ Almighty! we knew about it. Stand on the hearth, line us up in front of him, take his belt off, then – wallop.' He gestured, peopling the room with the three boys cringing, with the man collarless, brass stud gleaming at his throat, braces stretched, feet apart, toes gripping the rug and his boots propped against the fire irons behind him. 'He'd give it us on the legs, then, "Backsides," he'd shout and have another crack, us hopping about, but he could hit a moving target, drunk or sober, any day. Had to. Mind you, he'd of made up for it if he hadn't because sometimes we'd be sitting minding our own business and he'd give us a stinger as he passed. "What's that for?" we'd say. "For the one I don't know about," he'd say and go off laughing. No flies on Dad. We needed every one he handed out, and more. There wasn't much we wasn't up to.'

She was silent.

'It didn't do us no harm. If you've been up to summat you can expect to be belted. You've got to learn. And it took as much out of him as it did us. He'd work up a proper lather.'

'I'm not surprised. Perhaps it's a good job I don't go around caning my children.' But her face was unsmiling.

'Nobody asked you to teach. I can bring in enough.'

The comment was unthinking reflex. The issue had been settled before their child was born.

'You're not keeping on at that school now there's a baby on the way,' he had stated.

'I'm allowed two months off before, on full pay. I've enquired. After, I have to stay away for two months, but without pay.'

'Are you telling me you want to go back *after* she's arrived? Who'd look after her? Your place is here, in this house, when there's a babby, not dinning it in to other folks's kids.'

6

She was shocked. 'I can't give up teaching. It's my job. The Office let me carry on after I was married. I can't let the Chief Officer down.'

He had summoned her to him and taken great pains to explain why he had waived the ruling in her case: the school was settled with her; he was pleased with the standard and read out one or two sentences from inspectors' reports, though they were confidential; and, referring to a file on his desk, recalled that she had gained the highest marks in the County when she had taken the external certificate. She had felt flattered and honoured.

'That was all flannel,' Hubert said. 'What man would want to teach in this hole, and how many would put up with coming out here in all weathers, day in, day out?'

'I did.'

'On your bike! I wasn't going to have any wife of mine biking twenty-four miles a day, all told.' For that reason they had rented a cottage in the village when they married. She smiled. It was pleasurable to be cherished. Now he did the journey and his motorcycle had been their first expense. 'We'll see what's best for the bairn. She's not having her nose pushed out while you tent on other kids.'

Yet his words were only a pretence at authority. He had married a school teacher and for her to be less now would reduce him, lower his standing. Though that might bring compensations.

For even on the day that the news of his engagement scurried up and down the scaffolding and he was congratulated, ogled at, the object of a new kind of deference because of her, even on that day there had been a shadow. There in the teasing, in the subtle embarrassment of the men.

> Clicked with a teacher, has he? Thought he liked them fancy.

Where did you get off, Hube? Must have been a
    Friday
Down at the Drill Hall, him all toffed up.
That's where you clicked, then, is it? But had to
    keep his gloves on
Else he'd not get near her. And he'll need them
    again.
He'll never hang his gloves up! I mean them for
    dancing.
Nice bits of skirt down there, if you're not too
    faddy.
Don't give him more ideas, he's been faddy enough.
Watch what you're doing, mate, don't say we didn't
    warn you,
Or she'll have you in a white collar, soon as you're
    spliced.
Him in a collar! Best mind your p's and q's, mate.
Take my advice, lad, will you? Don't forget them,
As you passed on the ladder.

It took most of his wage packet in the pub that evening
to persuade them that he had not changed, but a distance
had been created.

Which, still, he enjoyed.

He'd got them going all right, no arguing about that,
looking at him out of their eye corners because he'd stepped
out of line. He knew what they were thinking but it didn't
signify, him marrying some'un as brought in money. Thought
the world of her, whatever they made of it, and proud of
her too.

'I can't give it up. It's my job,' she said. She was a
teacher. So she must teach. It was as simple as that.

Almost, because there was pride in her too, but like her,
contained. Teaching was her achievement. It had been
hard won and she had been required to sink so much in it

that to have given it up would have left her a blank, would have removed her identity.

So, when she had finished bathing her daughter and taken her to a neighbour, the image which had slackened only a little during her care became pronounced as she walked to the school, planning her day. She was a teacher. *The* teacher, her position acknowledged by the people she passed: a farm labourer raised his cap; a woman beating carpets paused and looked at her through the dust; an old man, self-elected sentinel, moved from her path. Their behaviour was cautious but it was not hostile. It gave recognition to what she was and that was enough. In her own village, once she had begun high school she had been someone eccentric and apart. Here, where no one shared her childhood, where at her approach no ghosts stirred from a tenting bush or a stump of wall, here her separation was inevitable and natural. It was also a measure of her success.

Although she was thus estranged she accepted the fact without reflection because she was not dispossessed. The unhurried movement of the seasons, the low fields stretched at the base of a vast sky which was given neither limit nor mystery by the interruption of hill or peak, these received her; the monochrome lives corresponded with her own. She walked between two rows of cottages down a private path by tradition permitted to the teacher, smelt the border of phlox and the laundered scent of clothes on the clipped hawthorn and watched her shadow ripple purple over lettuces and banks of potatoes. When she reached the lane she could hear the early children playing and knew by the sounds which games they were engaged in. As soon as they saw her, one ran to meet her and take her basket and immediately she had opened the padlock on the gate they spilled after her and went racing round the playground.

Unlocking the door of the school and crossing the narrow flagged cloakroom, Alice entered the classroom, its ceiling high pitched above cross beams, its walls unplastered and varnished a harsh green, lit by tall windows and unevenly heated by a derelict stove, crowded with cupboards and heavy bench desks. Built in the early years of state elementary education, it stood square and unrelenting, appropriate for the children of the labouring poor. And from evidence on walls and sills, the education was consistent with its setting: cardboard covered Stories from History, *Ivanhoe*, the poems of Tennyson, bean bags and hoops, spelling lists with the vowels in red, cards pinned on a chalk drawing – This is Rover, snout, tail, spot, whisker – stick men balancing on rungs as they recorded individual endeavour up narrow ladders; all sober rectitude but winked at by the sun running along a line of clean jam jars ready for the afternoon's painting and over clay-brown honey pots, plump and unglazed, capped with gold crocuses.

The room gave Alice poise and serenity. It was hers. She had made it her own and as she entered she looked round like one checking in a mirror and smiled to see the features steady and unchanged, their plainness made congenial by affection and use.

Outside her children played noisily as they waited to begin lessons, contained by the wall which Hubert had been sent to repair.

'Will you be here tomorrow?' she had asked the workman above the heads of the small ones who had gathered round inspecting his tools.

He straightened but did not touch his cap as he had that morning before observing her youth. 'No, I've finished. Just got to clean up, then I'll be on the next bus back.'

The children chorused disappointment. His presence had made the day festive. During play time they had mixed cement, learned how to use a trowel, had clamoured for piggy-backs and shown him their treasures. He enjoyed their attention hugely, swung a little girl round him till her skirt was a circular flange, and made a feint at an unguarded chest.

She was piqued by his easy success. 'Would you like to wash in the cloakroom?' and led him away.

Standing by her desk, she listened to him washing, heard his hands slapping and kneading lather on his face, the water tumbling back into the bowl, the snorts and splutters through the suds, then the sounds of the towel rolling on the pin, the spanks of it on his arms and the whistle rhythmic but soft because of the place. He had a zest, a gusto of the senses which powered his behaviour. It was as if he lived straight from his nerve ends.

'Thank you,' he said at the door of the classroom. 'Where do you empty the water?'

'On one of the gardens.'

'I watered a row of lettuces,' he reported. 'They looked thirsty.'

'We could do with some rain.' She wanted to delay him. For her, as for the children, his visit had been an event. 'It's been a long way for you to come, just to repair a wall. I informed the Office and Mr Higgs would have asked a local man, but the one who could have done it is ill.'

'It needs a man in the trade.' He looked away and saw her bicycle propped outside the porch door. 'That back tyre's looking a bit flat. I'll give it a pump up.'

He squatted down, fitted the nozzle over the valve, then pumping across a thigh, forced the air in with regular, controlled thrusts.

'Haven't I seen you somewhere before?' Over the curve of the mudguard he examined the pattern of her skirt and her fingers spread, flattening the folds. 'You live at the end of the village, near the bus stop.'

11

'Oh, no. I cycle here every day from Bainbridge.' It lay on the edge of his town.

'That's right. Now I've got you. I was on a job there a few months back. You're in that house on the corner, next to the rectory.'

She laughed. 'No, I'm in digs in Carlton Street.'

'You must have a double,' he said cheerfully as he stood up. He had gained the information he wanted. Because, he said to himself, she isn't a flirt. She didn't know what I was after. School teacher! She doesn't know a damned thing about it.

'I'll be going, or I'll miss that bus.'

Never had any truck with teachers, not since the day I left school. Best day in my life, that was. Dad brought me in a Guinness that night, said I could pay him back out of my first wage packet, pretending to be mean. I knew what he meant. First wage packet! She wasn't bad, though. Asked me in for a wash. Perhaps she doesn't like to see muck. Not that I was mucky, don't spread it on myself. That wall'll stand up a few more years, though it was laid like a dog's hind leg, and I gave that tyre a good pump up for her.

'How many miles is it to Bainbridge?' leaning forward to the driver.

Twelve. Why doesn't she bus it?

'What time's the next bus after the seven o'clock?'

Eleven, so she has to bike it. Anyway, she'll go sweeter now on that back tyre. Not a bad job she's got, if that's what you like. Your own boss. But water in buckets! At least at Burton Street we had a tap, old Wilkes standing with his cane while you used it; he couldn't half lay it on. I wonder if she can. She doesn't look like it, but you never know. Still, you could tell she's a teacher, the way she walks, stuck up, telling folks to watch out; all the same, I reckon she didn't want me to go. I'm not green. Gave her a chance, pumping up her tyre, but she didn't take it. It was for her to start; it's her school. Never get anywhere with her, too quiet; she laughed, though, when I said she lived next to the rectory. She looked nice when she laughed, not like a teacher, but I reckon it would take some doing, getting laughs out of her. She had nice ankles. I could see that when I was at the bike. But it would be hard work, spite of her hands pressing her dress and her holding her breath while I pumped, still as a mouse and her eyes watching as if they'd never seed anyone pump a tyre before. I'll have to give that a try again. And I know what some'ud say. 'Can I give you a pump up, Sweetheart?' 'Get away with you, dirty bugger.' Not this one though. I must want my head examining.

Two days later he left work early and was at the end of Carlton Street waiting for her to arrive home.

Chapter Three

'So you've come,' Mrs Livesey greeted. 'I can recognize you by the photo. I haven't touched anything. It's just as he left it. I don't want you to think I've been into his things. That's for his own. But I've been in to open the window in the morning and close it at night. Keeps down the must. I don't want that. So it was heart then, was it? I didn't think it'ud be anything else. A man like him, the only way he could go, with his heart. He'd be a bit offhand at times, we all have our moods, but when he got going he could make you laugh. Better than a tonic. But not as good as eight pints and a cuddle, he'd say. He didn't mean anything; it was only his way. He could tell a yarn. But I don't have to say that; you know as well as I do. The stories he would tell about folks in Drythorpe village, and take them off to a T! You should be on the telly, I used to tell him. But I oughtn't to be talking like this. It's that I can't believe he's gone. You'll be wanting to get on. I'll make you a pot of tea when you shout.'

She drew the door closed and left them standing together in the room never let to them or set out to give them welcome, and like children locked in for punishment they both watched the door until it was flush with the casing and then looked round, apologizing for their presence, for observing without permission private habits indicated in the still-life arrangements: a kettle and a mug containing an infuser for tea standing on the floor by the electric point; a handkerchief stained with snuff pushed down the arm of a chair; neat crescents of nail parings in an ashtray; socks, pegged down by the clock, hanging stiff and dry now from the mantelpiece; and on the table by the bed a glass eggcup half filled with grey water waiting to close over a single plastic eye.

At last, 'Better get on with it,' Michael said. 'I'll see to the clothes, bundle them up to take them along to Oxfam or the local vicar. There are the papers, too. Mrs Livesey said we would find all "his credentials" in a suitcase under the bed. Apparently he had told her where to look if she ever had to, and she was very careful to make it clear that she never had.' He paused but she did not comment. 'I don't mind if you prefer me to do that.'

She shook her head and knelt to withdraw the case. It was small, painted a commercial brown, the layers of compressed paper yawning at the corners like grey fungus and the catches pocked with rust. The contents slid about loosely as they moved – a few letters, a photograph album, several receipts thrown in arbitrarily, and a number of buff envelopes. Reading their titles, she laid them in chrono-logical order across the lid of the case: birth certificates; marriage lines; Hubert's apprenticeship indentures; Alice's teacher's certificate (1919); Hubert's club; my insurance; identity cards; Post Office savings book; NHS cards; then in another hand, Alice's death certificate God bless you darling and RIP.

'You see that?' Stella asked. The final envelope quivered in her open palm. 'As if there had been nothing else. Rest in peace! Why did he do it? Finding an envelope, writing, licking the flap. It's like a private burial. And it is so lonely. I should have tried harder. I should. No matter how I felt.'

Kneeling by her, he said, 'You did all you could,' before hearing the ambiguity. Half in apology and half in comfort he put his hand on hers. But she did not respond and he knew himself to be an intruder, attempting to interpose his warm flesh between her and her dead.

'I should have tried more,' she insisted, 'but I knew that he would regard any contact as a kind of collusion, so it was impossible once I understood what was happening to her and after she died. It was always impossible. Now he is dead.'

The first time he, too, had grieved. Now, regarding his hand spread over his thigh, he drew from this death nothing more than apprehension, the flinching possibility of his own mortality.

'Always the same,' she muttered.

'Not always the same. There were happy times.' He wished to be attended to. Exclusion was not merited.

'Yes, that's true. I tell myself that. Even the usual childhood fears were almost exciting when he was about. I used to be afraid of going to bed because the shadows from the candle were live things sliding in and out at me as the flame moved in the draught. When he knew, he brought the dog in and sent her into corners to root for goblins and when she didn't find any he said they had been scared off by the smell of her. I believed it and after that I liked to lie warm in bed watching the patterns from the candle on the wall. The snow in winter was better, though. He'd take me out on the sledge along tracks the bus had made, where the snow was packed and glassy, and he'd slip and roll into the untouched verges and let me sit on his stomach and rub snow into his hair and cram it into his mouth. Then he'd shake himself like a dog and we'd be off again. When we reached home he'd undress me in front of the fire, make two mugs of Oxo, two cubes in each mug, and we'd warm

16

our faces in the steam and keep checking whose nose would thaw out first.'

'He was at his best with children,' Michael attempted and disliked himself for the sterility.

'I want to remember what he was,' she pleaded. She was trying to salvage tenderness. She was trying to discover nooks in the dead man which she could accept without shame, in which she could curl and prove herself not orphaned. While the man beside her, looking into her dry face, wanted to crush away the disfigurement this death had caused. Yet he could not allow her deceit. 'You do remember. You remember very accurately all that he was.'

'Yes, I do.' She defied him. 'He was my childhood.'

'For Christ's sake,' he hissed, gripping her arm. He would not sanctify a space he could not himself fill. 'And what of her? What of Alice? What was he for her?' The roar and clangour of the man was in his ears; a woman with bloodless face turned her head. He felt the bone through her flesh. 'I'm sorry,' he said, and dropped his hand. The ghosts retired. He sighed. It seemed that the only way he could reach them and the passion which linked them and the woman at his feet was in the destructive manner of the dead man. No, he said to himself, better not to know than descend to that.

'You know how I think of her,' Stella said.

'I wonder why she married him, or why they ever stayed together.' It was a commonplace speculation concealing much. Do people ask the same about us? he thought, surprised, and decided that they did not. Their marriage was firm. Friends considered it ideal. But now he briefly questioned its careful serenity. His eyes following the handwriting of the dead, he momentarily envied them their anguish.

'She never said,' his wife answered. 'That would have

17

been disloyal, to her practically a sin.' She gathered up the buff envelopes and made them into a little stack on the floor. 'There isn't much to show for them both,' and continued to sort through the contents of the suitcase, grieving not at their death but for them living.

Downstairs Mrs Livesey had set a tray with cups and saucers and buttered scones. The hand-embroidered tray cloth, part of her bottom drawer and never before used, had been aired and she had polished her best china with a warm teatowel. The water in the kettle was kept boiling over a low jet and she was re-tidying the room briskly, but each time she approached the dresser she stopped and looked quickly towards the door. The narrow tape around the package had not been untied but, from lifting the broken corners, she had known what it held when she had taken it on impulse from the suitcase. Now she was left with it propped behind the hyacinth, but visible, accusing; and worse, a temptation. It was impossible to replace it later and then deny knowledge of its absence, and to carry it upstairs to them and confess was more than she could undertake. So she must burn it, and she thrust the sharp point of her iron poker under the coals, levered them up vigorously until the fire sprang through the upper layers, made a sudden grab for the packet, dragged off the tape and paper, and began to drop the letters one by one into the flames. But even separated, their bulk lessened in order not to stifle the draught, they would not be so easily consumed, and she was forced to squat before them with the remainder still weighing on her hands and watch the ink darken then shine before the leaves curled, broke and dropped their brittle fragments of words still glowing through the shimmering coals. Until, with a gasp of resignation, she did what she had purposed the moment she had found the bundle: unfolded a sheet and began to read.

She read them all, relished each one like a treat deferred, mouthed the concluding endearments with chaste pleasure as if they had been addressed to herself, and then paused, straining wistfully to hear the distant pulse of her own youth. She held the pages delicately at the edges, brushed the hearth rug with the back of her hand before laying the first down, and arranged the rest neatly on top, smoothing creases and pressing back folded corners. When she had finished she took the fire tongs, removed a piece of coal from the centre and placed the sheaf in the hole she had made. The flames stroked the edges, crept between the leaves, raised them in fiery layers, then drew back, and the letters sank down molten, welded together by the heat.

'There you are. Safe,' Mrs Livesey murmured. 'No wonder he kept them all these years. You were a clever young thing, but not hard, up with the lark to put on paper what you couldn't say the night before, courting, and you made him a good wife as promised, by all accounts. He never said otherwise. They're seen to now. I've seen as they don't get into the wrong hands,' she concluded piously, and, using the tongs, rolled back the cooling ember into its place.

Chapter Four

As soon as he was clear of the town he leant forward, flexed his elbows, gripped the tank with his knees, and let the throttle full out. She was a good bike and he kept her well greased and tuned. With the hedges clipped short and the land so flat on all sides, he could see if anything were coming for miles and could go full out in stretches, hardly slowing down for bends, the draught tossing his hair, midges bouncing off his goggles, and the wind tearing through his lungs.

Friday night, half-past four knock off, pay packets all round, and on the bike. Could have dropped Bill off at the bottom of Clasketgate, the old devil's been angling for a ride in the side car, fancies hisself stretched out like a lord, but if he won't ride pillion he's had his chips, nobody's muckying up that side car. Reserved for the babby.

The crossing gates ahead of him were closed and he swore at the necessity to slow down. If there were more traffic on these roads the keeper would open the gates between trains, not wait for demand. Somebody ought to tell the lazy sod; but it was none of his business. He kept his fingers round the horn until a face appeared at the kitchen window of the house next to the line.

. . . And would you believe it, he didn't budge! Just stood glegging through the glass, like he'd lost a quid and found a tanner. With the side car stuck on her, I couldn't push her through the side gate like I normally do, so I waved and pointed to the car, and the old bugger nodded and waved back. 'What you want?' I shouted. 'A bloody letter of application?' and he cocked his head as if he hadn't heard right. Deaf as well as incapable. God, I was mad. I jumped off the bike and started to open the big gates. That shifted him, but I had banged it to and was half-way across the lines before he was out, waving his arms and shouting. I hadn't noticed the signals. You never expect a train's coming, just because the gates is closed. But he didn't half move, I'll say that for him. I got him jumping. He unlatched the gate and held it as I squeezed round and got it closed as the train was coming round the bend. 'You silly bugger!' he says, and his face was white; near having a heart attack. 'What's up?' I says. 'You should've come out sooner. Do your job proper, not stand warming your ass in front of the kitchen fire while I'm here honking'. . .

It was Friday night. The fields on either side of him were level and unpresuming and he gave them not a moment's heed. His eyes on the lane rushing towards him, he rode on the rim of the world, feeling the throb of the engine under him and straddling its power.

Leaving the motorcycle outside the gate, he crunched down the ash path, let the dog off its chain and strode into the house.

'Where's that wife of mine?' he called and swept her onto his breast. 'You smell soapy. Been washing your hair? That's good because I've got a surprise. Hope it's dry by the time we've had tea. Don't want you to catch cold.'

'What is it?' She was pleased but as always a little anxious.

'Never you mind. It's pay day. Here.' He slapped the unopened wage packet on the table. 'Extra this week, with that bit of overtime. So we're off on the razzle. And how's my babby?' he demanded, scooping up the child. 'You been a good girl today and behaved yoursen so's Daddy can be proud of you? Has she, Joan?'

'Joan's waiting to be paid,' Alice prompted.

It had been his suggestion they employ Joan. 'I don't like the babby being lugged off down the street every day to be minded,' he had said. 'I like to think of her playing here, at home. Joan can clean up as well. I want a wife to come home to, not a scullery maid.'

'I can manage. It's bound to be hard work,' she expressed the expectations of her breeding. To be cherished was still a novelty. But she finally agreed, though apprehensive at inverting the rank of her birth and becoming an employer.

That did not bother Hubert. Inside his own kitchen, safe from workmates' observation, the act of paying Joan could be savoured and enjoyed and he emptied his wage packet onto the table, counted five shillings into her palm, folded her fingers over the coins, patted the fist and said, 'Now don't go blewing that all in one go.'

Joan nodded and blushed. 'I shan't have the chance.'

'Your time will come. I was twenty-one afore I was let look into my wage packet,' and he drew her into the porch.

Asking her to return in an hour to put the child to bed and remain there while he and Alice spent the evening in town, Hubert stood with an arm round her shoulder, squeezed her to him as each request was agreed to, and offered to fetch and take her home on the motorcycle as a treat which Joan, blushing once more, interpreted as a bribe.

'She's a good girl, even if she is a bit slow,' he commented.

'She's shy in front of you. She was one of my best girls, passed the first part of the scholarship the year we were married. I told you.'

'I've forgot.'

22

'Her father wouldn't let her go for the interview. I did my best to persuade him. Joan's a clever girl. She should have been given the chance of taking the second part, but Mr Thorpe wouldn't hear of it.'

'What more can you expect round here?'

Encouraged by his interest, she continued, 'It's always the same. I don't seem to get any further. She has brains. She could do better than this.'

'And she could do worse. There's things she'll need besides brains. I hope she's got them.'

She shrank from the knife resting steady on the rim of the plate and from the eyes looking at her, shrewd and quizzical. Regarding his hands calloused by the tools he had inherited, how could she describe the value to her of the course she had chosen? Education was her creed, derived from a mother whose period in service had taught the demeanour of gentility, the accepted fashion for laying the table and the privileges awarded to post-elementary schooling.

'Anyway, I get fed up. It's like you having a pile of bricks but not being allowed to use them.'

'That's different. There's not a deal else you can do with bricks, 'cept chuck them through winders.' He smiled and bent his head to his plate. There was no longer any need to hold her with his eyes. He was elated, for he had beaten her where she was the stronger, and his plans for the evening were no longer a gift but a lordly hand-out to be received with gratitude.

Which Alice gave him. It was thrilling, the idea of going into town for an evening, like being courted all over again, and she propped the flat-iron against the hearth bars so that she could smooth the creases from a stored blouse and squeezed her still damp hair between her fingers in the hope of fluting the straight bob.

Seeing which, he laughed. For it was Friday night – no one flogs hisself on Saturday morning – and he was king, laughing when she hurried to wash at the sink before him, laughing because there was overtime money on the table and in half an hour she would be behind him on the pillion, clinging to his belt, screeching out as they went round corners towards the queue at the pictures, the teasing dark inside and then the chips under a lamp. Everything as it had always been before miles of unlit empty lanes separated him from his bed.

As she began to clear the table, she was called to the front door.

'It's the last day of the month,' the man announced, coming into the kitchen. 'I'm sorry I didn't bring it to school first thing, only I was on early shift.' Taking an envelope out of his pocket, he removed a cheque, scrutinized it and placed it on the table. 'That's right.'

'Thank you, Mr Hennell.'

He waited for her to pick it up but she left it beside the notes and coins spilled from Hubert's wage packet. 'It's right. I checked against the salary claim. Allus do. You can't be too careful. Them clerks in the Office can easy make mistakes.'

'Thank you,' she repeated.

'Well, I'll be getting on. That's one job out of the way, at any rate,' then added comfortably to Hubert, 'Thar's all right for a bit, now.'

Saying farewell to Alice, he followed her to the door.

'The bloody cheek,' Hubert burst out, the door barely closed. 'What's he mean, I'm all right for a bit? Hinting I'm living off you. What's he think I do, getting on the bike every morning? Blewing it all on the horses, I suppose, not sweating my guts out to bring home a wage big enough to look after anyone I've got to, not like him, keeping his

24

palm greased for tips, "Can I carry your bags, Modom? Would you care for a seat by the window, Modom? Can I wipe your nose, Modom? Or your arse?" So I'm all right, am I? That's what he thinks.'

'It was only something to say. He didn't mean anything insulting.'

'You don't think so? You wasn't standing where I was. So it's all right by you, is it, if some candle-nosed LMS porter comes creeping up to me and gives me a piece of lip? You like that, do you? Puts me in my place?'

'I don't know what you're talking about. Flying off the handle like this . . . you're just being silly.' Disapproval made her voice prim.

'Don't you use that tone to me never again,' he said slowly. 'I'm not one of your kids, nor ever like to be.'

'There's no need to say that.' The situation had gone beyond her.

'What's he got to do with your wage, anyway?'

'Mr Hennell is Correspondent for the Managers. You know that. He sends my claim into the Office and they send him the cheque at the end of the month.'

'So him, and all the rest of the managers, know what wage you get! It's not right. A bloody railway porter seeing your wages! And every sodding person in the village will know! It's no business of theirs to know what you're pulling in. You want to create about it, tell them you want paying private or something.'

'I never thought of complaining.'

He grinned. 'You need me to look after you.'

Their glance touching, for a moment a sensation passed between them. She looked down, shy under his gaze, and began to shuffle together the money and cheque. Watching her, he was humiliated by the contrast between the soiled notes, the dull coins and the symbol of a closed privileged world; and he could find no way to vent his feelings, while her hair, light as feathers after its recent wash, stuck out in a fine gauze above her ears and the tip of her tongue showed nipped between her lips. His eyes shifted to his daughter.

And in an instant he had made up his mind.

'Here, how'd you like to go to the pictures, little lady? Your dad'll have to dress you all over again.'

Holding her raised arms, gloving his large hand in her dress, dropping it straight as a parachute over her head and signalling fingers, twirling her round, fastening the buttons, placing her hands on his head for balance while she stepped into knickers he stretched wide and round as her jerry, and all the time dismissing his wife's startled objections: yes, she was coming; no, it wouldn't do her any harm being up so late; yes, they'd let her in; of course he hadn't forgotten Joan. He would call in on their way past and tell her.

So Alice was punished and he turned his back on her, filled up the ladle and stood the child on a chair to watch him shave, hung his collar and tie round her neck and gave her a beard and whiskers of lather and bright cheeks with the promise of an organ coming up through a trapdoor and lighting with all the rainbow colours. While Alice, as she waited to use the sink, stood at the edge of their shared happiness, disappointed at the altered plan; and because she had been taught that some emotions are unnatural and therefore shocking and forbidden, those she felt as she watched them together were modified to disapproval at his spoiling the child.

It was not until they were leaving that, closing the flues, she saw the flat-iron still propped against the bars.

But once out in the lane with the evening sun sealing the odours of the day and the fields tranquil as light drained through the grass, she was more content, receptive to the possibility of enjoyment; and he, no longer even remember-

26

ing his reason for bringing the child, called for his wife's help as if she had never been excluded, stuffed the child into the side car as she held back the flap, teased her as she fumbled with a stud, caught her up where she stood and toppled her onto the pillion, smoothed her skirt behind her calves, laughing, boisterous, noisy, kicking the starter and leaping into the saddle with as fine a bravura as a hussar leading the charge.

Because it was Friday night and her arms were round his waist and Stella was cuddled up in the side car, and its wheel spun loose soil and pebbles into the hedge. While, keeping the cycle at the centre of the shallow camber, he rode on the crest of his world.

Chapter Five

'Hello, love, we're here,' Alice told him, leant to him kept upright by pillows and pressed her lips into his hair.

He jerked back, his head scarfed by the thick wad. 'Hey, what's come over you? I've still got this.' His mouth stretched and showed teeth but without supporting expression his intention was ambiguous and she shivered. 'Don't pay no attention to them,' he cooed. 'After all I've said they'll be sorry if it isn't a rare 'un.'

She looked quickly along the double row where faces mostly blinkered turned and bobbed and strained on taut necks for the wilful chinks of sounds, then she bent lower and kissed him hastily on the lips. Separated from other features, their warmth and eagerness chilled her.

Disappointed, he slid his hand along the starched coverlet. Then it rose and circled until it found the girl. 'You give your old dad a big smacker,' he said; after which, 'I'm pleased you've got your school blazer on,' running a finger along the braid. 'The way I've swanked to some of the lively ones opposite, I reckon they think it's all tales, so I'm pleased you didn't leave it off. It'll show them.'

Beyond Sister's table in the centre, the upright piano and the dahlia-filled jars, the lively ones sat with their blanked-out faces pointed to the door, waiting for a touch to start at.

Turning her back on them, Alice drew her chair nearer his bed in an irrational impulse to shield him.

She was surprised by this new feeling though it was only natural when he was propped up here and in many ways helpless; he would have to have things done for him, even be fed – there was a tea mark on the collar of his pyjama jacket below his ear, as if the nurse had slopped it – but this idea that she must look after him, stop him from being hurt, had started last week when it happened. Not because of the mess his face was in, but because of the way he was, so frantic, grabbing her when she ran in after the bang and holding her arms so that it took her all her time to get free long enough to find some clean rags, and crying to her not to leave him, and hanging onto her belt when she tried to get to the door and call Mrs Shorthose. It was the way he was that had been such a shock, more than his face covered with ash and slime and blood and making a sort of sling with a piece of rag to scoop up the jelly hanging on his cheek in a slick of tissue and froth and pushing it back into the socket. In the end that had been no good but it wasn't that which had been so awful. It was the clinging and whimpering and crying that all he could see in the other eye was red and yanking on her arm and leaving blood and bits on her sleeve as if she had been injured, too. She could put up with that and the blood running into his mouth and down his sideburns and that water that had spurted onto his trousers from the tear bag; it was him going to pieces that had been so upsetting. She had been thinking about him all week, not in the way you do when you are courting but weighing him up, which was dreadful and she'd never tell a soul, but she knew now why it had seemed so wrong, him behaving like that. It was because it was always him that took charge and now he was making her the one, not only then, but as if he had always wanted it, kneeling on the hearth rug holding his face and blubbing like a baby that

29

he was finished if she left him, that all he had ever had was her.

Yet he had always said that what she needed was him to look after her. That was his way of putting it: you need me to look after you. Which had made her laugh first time but she did not laugh again because she could see it hurt his feelings. In any case, you can't say it isn't nice, having someone to care for you; it was his way of showing he cared. Her family never talked like that and they didn't go about hugging and squeezing as he did. He always wanted his arm round her, not just because it is the thing when you are courting, but because he liked to be close. 'You're going to marry me,' he had said, 'because you can't stop yourself. The first time I clapped eyes on you I knew you were the one that was going to marry me. And she knows, I said to mysen. She's had her eyes skinned for someone like me to take care of her. I'm just the job.' Then he pressed his teeth into her lips but she could not tell him that she preferred his first kind of kissing when he was not trying to persuade her, when he held her face between his hands and kissed her gently as if he were scared, too. That was how it ought to be, not hurting, not the kind of kissing which made her tremble. He had laughed when she trembled, sort of cocky and pleased with himself, and she remembered what her mother had once said, 'It's what a man does to a woman that I can't forgive and then blames her when she's carrying.' She had wished it could always be the first kind of kissing.

She watched him as he sat with one hand over the girl's, gripping her wrist, smiling, telling her jokes about the nurses.

He was a good father. They always got on well together. Sometimes, seeing her when she was a baby, jumping round her dad, looking so glad and lively, it made you thank your lucky stars for her sake. It was something not many had;

she'd never had it herself. She didn't find it easy, messing about as he did, and as he said, having the school she hadn't much spare time. Though she could have made some. They often did things she would have liked to join in with and surely it must be possible to learn to play as much as to work if people will be patient. So she would have made the time if they had asked her.

'What did the doctor say this morning?' she asked.

'I'm doing champion. He says if I behave mysen – your dad's got to behave hissen! – I can have these off by the end of the week. Not before time, either. I don't know why they have to bandage them both. Keeps us in bed, I suppose, out of mischief. When they let me out we'll go on the spree, celebrating. Best excuse I ever had as never wanted one! And there's another thing. Lying here, playing blind man's buff, I've been going over the antics you and me used to get up to, Sweetheart, and I remembered the kite. We haven't had it out for years. We'll give it an airing. There's nothing can beat that kite once it gets going. Like the time we took it out on your birthday. It must've knowed.'

'The kite's still hanging in the cubby hole, isn't it, Stella? We'll get it down, Hubert, and give it a wipe over. It's like you to be thinking of taking Stella out when it's you who are the patient.'

'What else is there to think about? I've nothing else to do all day. Did me a power of good, remembering that kite. So get it down, Sweetheart, and give it a wipe over and we'll have a rare old time one night when I'm out. Best kite I ever made if I'd of made any others.'

He was leaning into her and his face was turned where he imagined hers to be but, wrongly assessing the angle, he spoke past her and into the ward. The girl, embarrassed, shrank back and looked away.

31

It would not be so bad if he didn't keep saying it. If he didn't speak so loudly so that everyone can hear. You can't see whether they can hear because you can't see their eyes, but they look as if they are listening. If he would only stop saying it I could look and Mum wouldn't think I was mardy. I can't look at him when he goes on like this. If I did, I'd cry. I don't like him to see me cry, not now. I didn't mind once, when I was young, but now I don't want him to know. He would say he knew why and he couldn't; because no one, not a single solitary human being in the whole wide world, could ever know. I shouldn't be able to stop myself crying if I looked at him because it wasn't the way he says it was. He never noticed how I was nearly crying after he laughed. I couldn't help saying what I did, because the kite looked so nice standing on its tail with its shoulders bobbing, and it just came out: If you let it go would it keep going up and fly right through the clouds and keep on and on by itself and never come back? That's what made him laugh. He laughed so much it nearly choked him and he went on about how I'd be the death of him one of these days, the things I said, talking about letting the kite go after he'd put so much work into it. I didn't mean that really. I was trying to stop him messing about with it, racing backwards and forwards to make it curve and swoop because he said he had to put it through its paces. I wanted to go home after he had laughed but it was ages before he gave up and then he stopped at The Fox on the way back, saying he needed a pint and he'd see if I was clever enough not to let anyone pinch the bike while he was inside. I could have gone round the back where they have a swing and some rabbits but I didn't because I was scared to leave the bike, he was so cross. He wasn't cross with me until we met Mr Hennell who had asked whether I was taking the scholarship and said it would be nice for Mum if I passed and that if I rode my cycle to the station in the mornings he'd see that I was all right until I could look after myself. When we got home I was so cold I went upstairs for a cardigan and there was shouting though it wasn't Mum's fault that she hadn't been there to see I didn't catch cold. She had not been able to come with us since we'd had to pack the kite in the side car to go to Longholm football pitch, when we could have flown it in Shorthose's field, but he said there were too many nosey parkers about for that. I put the kite in the cubby hole while they were arguing. I had looked forward to it so much, but it was spoilt.

'I don't think I shall be able to, Dad. There's homework.'

'Get away with you! You'll not put homework before your old dad! We'll have that kite up higher than she's ever been before. I'm going to put a new reel on. Which reminds me. I'll nip round the day I'm let out and have a word with the lads and collect my club.'

'I went in yesterday,' Alice told him, 'and spoke to Mr Brough. Everything was in order.'

'The missis was in last Sat'day,' they greeted. They were uncomfortable, keeping their eyes from his patch. 'You've struck gold there, Hube. Had no more'n a few words with Mick and she had the club dividends off pat. You'd have expected her to be stuck up, being what she is, but she weren't. Mind you, she kept her distance; that's only right. But not stuck up. She brought the little gal. Of course, we knew who it was the minute we set eyes on her. I reckon she comes up nice on a photo but Mick doesn't think so; he says they take all the colour out of her.'

'She's got plenty of that.'

'Thought you might drop in. The missis said they was letting you out today and she was asking some'un coming in to market to drop your togs in.'

It was different from what it should have been. He had

meant to surprise them, show he was just the same as ever, get them laughing like old times: 'I can tell you a few about one little nurse', but he felt wrong, standing in his Sunday best with them lined up in a row and Bill's head poking up from the back as if he'd seen a ghost; more like one himself, his cap and moustache covered with plaster. He must have started on the downstairs already.

'Anyway, you'll be all right. The boss says it don't make no difference. You can have your job back.'

'I never bloody gave it up.'

'Well, no, you're right there. It was only in a manner of speaking. When we got the news we thought things was worse than they are – you know how folks talk – and we all thought it had got both, but seeing it's just the one, it's not so bad. You'll be carrying on much the same.'

'How'd you mean, much the same? I'll be carrying on as bloody usual. There's nowt wrong with me. One dicky eye don't put me in St Dunstan's.'

'All right, keep your hair on. Calm down, will you? Nobody's said give him his cards. It's a miracle how some people manage with just the one.'

'I'm telling you there's nothing I could do I can't do now. You don't believe me? You want me to prove it? Right, fetch that dart board out and I'll show you. Anybody lend me a set of arrers? She didn't think to swop mine over to this jacket. All right. What's it to be? All in top or shall I go for the old treble nineteen? Right, I'll do that. I'll drop three in a bed as sweet and snug as a bug in a rug.'

Well, the crafty old devil, he damn near did it.
You mustn't take on so, what more can you expect?
The first didn't amount to much but the second
wasn't far out,
And number three would've gone in if it hadn't
hit the wire.

34

Hey, did you hear what Bill says? He's a great one
    for trying:
You'll mebbe see better when they've fitted you a pot
    one.
So long as it isn't cracked.
Look, it's a thing to get used to and it might be a
    blessing;
With one eye out of action they'll not call you up.
All right, let it be, then, I'm sorry I said it,
But it's coming all right, spite of what they give
    out.
The boss had a letter about putting the Raf in
The other side of Grantby and very hush hush.

In spite of the sun he felt cold as he waited at the bus
stop. Standing by the curb, his suitcase between his feet
and the thick dressing wedged under the shade, he knew he
was conspicuous. Usually he liked to be noticed. He
enjoyed their eyes on him. He would hold his back straight,
draw in his stomach, flex his fists inside his pockets to feel
the muscles running up his arms, and would look round
him, knowing he was observed, favourably assessed.

But the attention he was attracting did not flatter.
Waiting for the bus, his large bleb pink and shining and
hard as a pantomime pate with cottonwool frizz teased out
at the edges, he was an object to be examined surreptitiously.
He was exposed, at risk, buffeted by eyes; and those he
could not see he sensed more acutely than the eyes known,
and if he swung round to confront them there were always
others out of sight, beyond the arc of his vision, clustered in
that great segment of darkness and revolving with it behind
his shoulder as he turned his head.

This solid shadow he carried with him when he stepped
out of the sun and into the dim bus, a black wedge which
radiated from his side and cut him off. Only by moving his

head like an animal searching for scents could he see the passengers' faces, and he picked out neighbours returning from market, glanced at them quickly and away without show of recognition or pleasure. Because he was inferior. Abnormal. While they watched him sidelong, prying, acquisitive, and jostled for gossip about a creature who had always disappointed their practice of rebuff. Clumsily he left his seat and sat in a corner where, next to the window, his burning flesh was sheltered from the gazers within.

There, a few inches from the glass, his face looked back at him as the bus passed out of the sunlight down a close tunnel of dense hedges and trees, but these ceased; his image became diffused, a botched phantom against the open fields, a few ghostly blurs among the green acres. Thus without a reflection, companionless, he looked out, saw hoof-pitted mud and litter of thistles and dung and thought of neat Sunday parks with lawns suavely mown for flir-tations; he looked at the sporadic farm houses flanked by pump and lean-to closet and remembered: the night streets fairy with incandescent cones, the rainbow streams along the gutters, the trams decked with faces and lights like holiday steamers, the glow-worm cigarettes down alleys, the greased smell of scraps at the Friday night butcher's, the beer smell swirling like fog round the pub yard and on the breath of men who said his dad was coming, the sticky band of his dad's trilby over his eyes. And still peering for the memory, the glass filmed with his breath, he made out faces at the roadside, faces of men who raised their caps to the bus, who took as their pattern for sleep and waking that of the beasts they tended, and as their occasion for leisure the day trip to the seaside organized by their chapel; men whose few words, like their lives, were spent on weather, animals and crops; who were alike frugal in love and fellowship.

But that was no matter; he had them taped. By God, you

36

could get some fun out of them. You could tell them anything and they'd take it all in. Like the time he did old man Shorthose's boots. The lads at work liked that one. Damn near busted their guts laughing.

. . . I could hear them coming up the lane, creak, creak, like a strip of tongue and groove Mick's seed to, and I says to him, 'Why don't you get them boots oiled?' and he says, 'I'm sorry if it's werriting you, Maister; they are a bit on the noisy side, but I'm hoping they'll quieten down when I've got them broke in. But for mysen, it isn't the squeak so much as the pinching. I can't seem to get topside of them.' 'Here, give us hold,' I said, 'I'll settle it,' and when I'd got my hands on one I said I'd have to keep it for a day or two, so he might as well leave the other as well. He hummed and hawed because I reckon he didn't fancy going home in his socks, but handed it over in the end, and went off. End of the week he comes round to collect and there and then puts them on and says, 'Them's a treat, Maister. There's still the noise now and again, but the pinch is gone. Thank you kindly. I appreciate this and I shan't forget it, never you fear.' Then he asks me what I done. I hadn't done a sodding thing, of course, since I stuck them behind the back door, but I spun him a yarn about hanging them in the soft water butt, hammering them out, drying them and rubbing hare grease into them. 'That's the answer,' I says, 'the hare grease. My dad got if off a Froggy at Wipers in the war. They eat it round those parts but my dad wanted it for his boots.' His mouth was hanging open wide enough you could have stuffed a brick in it. I got rid of him and thought namor of it, but that wasn't the end of the story. You'll never believe what's coming. A couple of weeks after, I'd just brought the new bike home, not half swanking it up the lane, and I'd propped it up inside the wash house and he comes to the back door, asking if he can borrow some hare grease to rub into a pair of boots some'un's got on the market for his missis. I couldn't very well refuse so I scouted round inside and came up with some grease for my rod, mixed it with a dollop of cochineal, and slapped it in a little jar. He was so grateful it would have made an undertaker laugh and I went back in to clean up. I hadn't been long standing in front of the mirror when I catched sight through the winder of summat moving in the wash house and I was out like a shot in my muck and lather and braces flapping, but quiet, meaning to catch the bugger red handed. And I did. Who d'you reckon it was? Old man Shorthose, bent over puffing and panting, rubbing that grease into the seat of my new bike! 'What the bloody hell you think you're doing?' I shouted and he jumped up like a kelly then stood there with his mouth open as if I'd gone off my rocker. I didn't half give him a mouthful; he'd got me so worked up I was near as nothing putting a fist in his kisser, and when I stopped, do you know what he said? He was *surprised* I was put out because he was only trying to make my seat as soft and comfy as I'd made his boots. Can you credit it? The poor sod really believed all that twaddle about the grease. You have to feel sorry for them, being so ignorant; they've never known anything better. Oh, yes, I got the grease off. Eventually. And when he was going, he said, 'I don't want you to think, Maister, that I don't know what I'm doing. I have my thoughts, and after you had troubled yourself with my boots I owed you something.' How d'you like that? Anyway, I must have put him off polishing for life because he went without the grease. I suppose he decided his missis's feet could stay pinched . . .

They had laughed a treat at that. They often asked for it again. One of them only had to say, 'Old Shorthose's boots' or 'Lend us a dollop of hare grease, Hubert,' to set them all off. They were a good bunch of mates.

With the sun full on him, he shivered.

All he had intended to do was show himself, prove that he was just the same as ever, that nobody could get one up on him, gammy eye or not. And he would have done it if he had had his own darts.

They had stood in a crescent, their eyes jumping from him to the unpinned board, gabbling advice and sympathy. He did not want that. He did not want their condescension, and gradually their faces had receded until he was alone on the other side of the water-filled trench, stubbing his feet against the rubble of the site, left to go home.

Home, where the back door was open but no one to welcome him.

'I should've thought you could've been here when I got back. It isn't much to ask.'

'I couldn't let them out early,' she said, her arms round his neck. 'Not when I closed for the whole day after it happened. Mr Hennell saw to it. He phoned the Office.'

'Well, he would, wouldn't he? Where's Enid?'

'You know it's her afternoon off. I didn't think you would mind if she went as usual.'

'It don't matter. I've seen mysen home, haven't I? You can't do more than you have when there's the school to see to. It has to come first.'

She was suddenly tired. 'You're having a joke. You know that nothing comes before either of you. You both come first,' and rubbed her forehead against his cheek.

Below the packed shield the other cheek itched for her touch but none came. 'I suppose we have to be thankful for small mercies. We mustn't grumble if it jumps into first place now and again,' deliberately misunderstanding her reference to their daughter.

All she could say was: 'That's not fair. You shouldn't say such things.'

'What things? I'm only saying what's right. And don't think I'm blaming you, making sure you don't put a foot wrong with the high-ups at the Office. You'll mebbe be glad of that, if this lot with Hitler comes off, having something coming in. Because they'll not have me in the Army with this, and who knows what I'll get put into, probably some flea-bitten job they pay you for in tiddly winks.'

He was holding her firmly for she was not to slip away from him as they had; but he kept his head half turned, as much in pretence that he could hide his dark side from her as in shame.

That night as he got into bed he said, 'I'll take the shade off after a bit.'

'There's no need. It can't be comfy.'

'It's not nice to see.'

'That's my look out.'

Shy as a virgin, he took off the patch and laid it on the chair by the bed head. 'It won't look so bad when the bruising's gone,' he apologized. 'Then it won't be so puffed up neither and the lid'll close proper so you won't see the red.' Then, 'It's nice being home. I could as near as nothing squeeze the breath out of you. And by the feel of you it's a good job I'm back. You need me to keep you warm. There's still things I'm good for, spite of what they say about the Army not having me – while they're handing out bent flights. You need me to keep you warm all right. It beats me how you could manage without me to look after you.'

Listening to the repetition of the familiar words, it was as if she were hearing a code which she at last understood but must never openly translate.

Chapter Six

'It doesn't really matter if he thinks that,' she would say to herself. 'It's what he wants. I don't suppose it does any harm, though it still doesn't seem right, letting him – it's like lying – and I wish I wasn't all the time expected to pretend.'

But there were demands Alice could not anticipate. She did not guess why Enid gave in her notice.

'I've got to finish working for you, Mrs Gourley. I've been talking to Mam and she thinks it's for the best.'

'Why Enid? I thought you were happy here.' It was six years since Enid had replaced her sister on her marriage and though the younger girl was timid and reticent, she and Alice enjoyed a constrained fondness.

'Oh, I am. You mustn't think I'm complaining. I wouldn't do that. It's that Mam thought, as things are, I ought to do something else. I'll go into munitions, mebbe.'

'I see. Well, I suppose I'm lucky to have had you these last years when you think about it, and Stella is getting on for sixteen, after all. She ought to be doing her share of the jobs. But I've grown used to having you, Enid. You are almost one of the family.'

'Yes.' The girl blushed, her fingers revolving a package inside the pocket of her apron. 'So I want you to have this back. I shouldn't have taken it. I knew he had been making it for Stella, but he was so pressing.'

Alice folded back the paper against her palm. Inside the small box, resting upon a compressed froth of cottonwool, was a brooch in the shape of an aeroplane.

'You mustn't do this when Mr Gourley has given it to you. He can always make another for Stella if she would like one. You will hurt his feelings. You don't usually return presents.'

'This wasn't Christmas or my birthday.' The girl could hardly speak. 'So it seems wrong, taking it. I don't want to finish here and leave you thinking I'd been forward. I didn't ask for it. Please, Mrs Gourley, take it back.'

Though distressed by her appeal, she was determined it should succeed. For the first time seeing her as a woman, Alice was perplexed with uneasiness which was oddly connected with the brooch.

Putting that from her on top of the dresser, she agreed, 'I'll explain to him. I hope it isn't too bad working at Marshall's.' She was unable to be more optimistic. She knew nothing of it but she had seen photographs in newspapers, women with bold faces and hair ridged with curlers under head scarves, linked in the palais glide between the factory gates. They seemed assured of their purpose and ruthless, their gaiety frightening; she felt guiltily thankful that her part in the war was more drab and solitary. 'You'll come and tell us how you are getting on, won't you? We shall want to hear, and if there is ever anything I can do,' but left the sentence unfinished for the young woman was looking away and shaking her head.

The gesture puzzled her and was recalled several times during the following months when Enid failed to visit them, but it remained unexplained until: 'No one's telling me there was nowt in it.' Craning over the counter towards someone cutting up lard in a cubby behind, the woman did not hear Alice come through the open door.

'No smoke without fire. Her mam didn't think so, either, the fust time – went running across the field to Glad Jay in a pickle and not time to say how do to the maister at the bus stop.'

She was cut short by the wife of the shopkeeper who, coming forward with the lard, saw Alice and addressed her very deliberately over the speaker's shoulder. The customer waited until Alice had replied then turned and, tight with discomfort, said, 'Excuse my back, Mrs Gourley, I didn't knowed you was there.'

Even without the reference to Gladys Jay, Enid's neighbour, Alice would have known whom they were speaking of; intuition leapt over deduction and she stood cold and apart, fearful of all that swelled unsaid across the counter of the watching shop. She made her purchases while the other remained, frankly waiting until she could resume the gossip Alice had interrupted, and she suffered the two women to pack her basket though she was breathless with panic to get away from them. Their manner was, as always, respectful and a little deferential, but now she noticed a faint quizzical expression on their faces, strangely contrasting with something else. For they helped her out of the shop as solicitously as if she had been lamed.

Trembling, but walking at her usual pace, she went on to the school, repeating what she had overheard, finding that it gave content to the talk of women at gates whose words in recent weeks had parted at her approach then closed again behind her; discovering that the name, Enid, gave substance to the sounds which had bulged behind cupped hands as she passed; and seeing in stares the examination of how she bore something still to her unknown. When she reached the school she let herself in quickly, made straight for her desk and stood by it panting, but gradually her breath was quietened by the orderly, known room, and as

43

the children came in and took their places she resumed her habitual balance. The enclosed day held her safe from questioning gazes and the voices she heard were of children chanting, singing, whispering or quarrelling, to her no threat. By the end of the afternoon as she led the prayers, the conversation in the shop had receded behind the sun-bleached room where her children stood before her bowed over their hands.

So she was able to ask, 'How's Enid getting on, Desmond? She hasn't been to see us since she left.'

Last of Enid's siblings, Desmond Thorpe had only two more years at school and Alice would not be sorry to see him go. He was precociously grown and unco-operative, longing for the open fields which did not need this sissy female schooling. In the last months she had thought wryly that the punishment his father had advised and carried out unnecessarily on his brother fifteen years earlier might have been better saved for Des but, the youngest by many years, he was spoilt and allowed to go unchecked.

Her question startled him. He was at first embarrassed, then sly. 'She's doing. She says Marshall's won't be so bad mebbe when she's used to it.'

He was accusing her. Outside the sun shone but in the dusk of the cloakroom the boy was putting her to a test, doing it with a grin that was prurient and calculating. Leaning back against the wall, she felt one of the iron pegs grate upon her spine.

'I hope so. It must be hard, working in a factory, but she knows she is doing her bit. Please ask her to drop in. We miss seeing her.'

In answer he jerked his head and gave a mocking snort, then keeping his eyes on the sun-covered lane, he pushed through the children to the open door.

There was nothing she could do. It was impossible to call

him back and demand an apology, for, the gossip and manner of the women returning to her in the wake of his answer, she felt defensive and harassed by undefined menace. She went back to the classroom.

It was the end of the day. Everything had been tidied and the room, neat but dusty, waited for the caretaker. Paintings were spread drying along the top of a cupboard; scrubbed ink wells stood in a line on the table; the slate with its painted columns for morning and afternoon attendances had been wiped ready for the next day; the sun shone on the varnished curves of the desks' iron frames. The room was tranquil, warm and unconfused, but for once its comfort was limited. While it was still unchanged, there was a noise of scratching at the base of its grass-hooped walls. It was faint but persistent and scraped at the peace.

At home Alice fetched in water, filled lamps and did the other jobs once Enid's and which would become heavier as the summer passed. Tidying the mantelshelf, she picked up the box Enid had given her and which had remained there as an object to be dusted ever since she had returned it to Hubert. The aeroplane winked up at her through its mimic cloud of cottonwool. It confirmed the women's talk but, refusing to make this explicit, she replaced the lid and tucked the box behind the candlestick. A few minutes later she went back, picked it up, dropped it into her apron pocket and carried it upstairs furtively as if she were watched. There, fearful of its meaning, she hid it away.

It was in a corner of the suitcase and her daughter picked it up and opened it upon her palm.

'That's rather pretty,' Michael said. 'It reminds me of something.'

'It should remind you of a Lancaster bomber.'

'No; years ago. On a dress. Haven't you one the same?'

'Mine is a Wellington.' She saw him grinning at her exactness. 'Well, we lived so near aerodromes, we could hardly avoid knowing.'

'Of course, your bit of the war.' A conscript before maturity, he assumed the right to mock. 'And his, too, I suppose. No doubt that was why he made the brooch.'

'It was a craze, but he certainly got the aluminium off the aerodrome.'

He had come behind her and, stretching over her shoulder, had placed the piece of metal in the middle of the page. 'How's that coming on?' he had demanded proudly. Intense heat and violent impact had sculptured the little lump into a cone of welded folds serrated at the edge. Bounded by heavy scores, a shape was jutting out of the surface. 'It's from that crash. I picked it up afore the salvage took over. What d'you think of it?'

'I don't honestly think it will ever get off the ground, Dad.'

'That's a good 'un! You can't half keep a poker face on you when you're about to crack one. Like your mother; never know what she's thinking. But you've got more than enough of your old dad in you, spite of your old-fashioned look now and again. I know; I've seen it.'

He clamped an arm round her shoulder and hugged her to him. Against her face his pullover was warm with the slightly abrasive smells of putty and plaster which had accompanied their romps when she was a child.

'What's this you're reading? One of your school books?

"Pillowed upon my fair love's ripening breast,
To feel for ever the soft fall and swell,
Awake for ever in a sweet unrest,
Still, still to hear her tender-taken breath,
And so live ever – or else swoon to death."'

He read it laboriously, missing the cadences with which Miss Carey had entranced them. 'It's a bit strong, isn't it? Not what we used to call Poetry, when it got a look in with old Wilkes, too busy caning, but I remember how Horatio kept the bridge. Used to like that. Couldn't half let that rip.'

At her side not cushioned by his bulk she could feel Miss Carey's distaste. 'It's a love poem.'

'I can see that! And you have to give it him, he comes right out with it. Look at that.' He ran a finger under "fair love's ripening breast". 'Not what you could say to the chaps at work but I suppose all right for him, being a Poet, though it makes you think she was a bit on the young side for that sort of thing.'

Encouraged, she could afford to smile. If she could make him understand he might not be subject to Miss Carey's disapproval. 'He was young, too, Dad; only twenty-five when he died.'

'Then you can't expect anything else. He don't know enough about it, else there'd not be all this swooning to death. That's pansy. When you're in love, you're alive. You're king. You don't go around swooning. I tell you, he doesn't know the half of it,' and with a strong flourish he bent forward and swept the book along the table.

For a moment they were both still. Then she pushed herself free of his grasp and pulled the book towards her. 'I think he does. I think it's beautiful.'

'Goodness me, girl, you don't cry at a poem. That's morbid. You don't want to be thinking about dying at your age.' He glanced at the lump of contorted metal. But the pilot had not been his son. 'Come on, put it away now and take your dad on in a game of darts. It'll keep your right arm supple and give you practice in mental arithmetic.'

'No, thanks, Dad. I think I would rather read.'

'That's all right. It was only a thought. Every man to his tastes. I'd rather play darts myself,' but his face was gaunt.

Frightened, she tried to make amends. 'What will it be when it is finished? By the way the tail is shaping, I'd say it's going to be a Wellington bomber,' making the mistake deliberately to entice him to forgiveness.

He shook his head, then hearing someone approach, kept his blank profile to her as he looked towards the door. 'Why, it's Enid. Just the girl we need,' and both his hearers flushed at the winced affability. 'What sort of aeroplane do you think this is? It's for Stella. She thinks it's a Wellington.'

Forced to take part, Enid stared at the metal. 'I don't really like to say. I suppose if you weigh up these little points, they're meant for two tail fins, so it'll be a Lancaster.'

'Now that's just what I wanted to hear. You're a proper mate, Enid. There's no need to tell me you keep your eyes open; you don't have them buried in books morning, noon and night,' adding in a dull way, 'I meant it for a brooch.'

Uncomfortable at the comparison, Enid tried to find a neutral topic. 'Alan Cook at Marshall's gets little brooches made out of silver thr'penny bits and sixpences. They squash them on a machine. They're nice. Little Spitfires. He says he'll make me one.' She blushed. 'If he does, I'll show it you.'

Her offer delighted him. Life ran in his speech again as he wondered whether Alan would rough one out for him to polish and solder onto a tie pin, as he invited her to a game of darts, as he brushed aside her excuses, as he persuaded her that she would find learning the game easy under his instruction, as he hustled her in front of him, repeating his compliment on her observation and knowledge of practical affairs.

While Enid looked anxiously at the other girl left sitting by the table, her fingers splayed over the pages of an open book and from whom he kept averted his sighted eye. Only the fixed other regarded her, its unaltering expression given false life by a nerve which flicked through the lower lid.

'It is a Lancaster,' she said, crouched over the case and looking up at the man who was her husband. 'He intended it for me. I wonder why he didn't give it to me.'

'You have the other.'

'Yes, the Wellington. That's odd, too, though I don't remember thinking at the time that there was anything strange about the alteration.'

She lifted the brooch out of the cottonwool and examined the neat solder which fixed the aeroplane to the pin. 'It's quite a work of art, but I wish I hadn't found it. It has an atmosphere. It is part of those years and I don't like them recalled.'

'They weren't so bad for you, Stella. Even the aerodromes in your part of the world weren't attacked, were they? The war hardly made any difference to life in your village.'

'It did to ours. At least, what happened during that time did.'

He knew now what she referred to and once again he was jealous of what bound her to her two dead. For though he distrusted this passion, and had no wish to share it, he was filled with a sense of loss.

Watching his face, she said gently, 'I can't help it, Michael. I have tried not to think about it. It would be easier, I think, if I could explain it, but there was so much I did not see – just as he didn't. I can't even explain this brooch. Do you know, it suddenly reminds me less of him than of Miss Carey.'

'Does it flatter her?'

'Because we created a myth for her after someone had

49

reported seeing her cycling near Digby aerodrome. After that, she became Digby Doll and spent all her free time peddling her wares from hut to hut, the cycle being an indispensable item after that rotten pun which never failed to bring us all near to hysterics. I don't know how my behaviour struck her at the time since, as I've told you, I had had that crush on her.'

'Which you'd grown out of, I'm pleased to say.'

'I think you would have been fitted in somewhere.'

'Don't be filthy. There are some parts of life where democracy does not attract at all.'

'Imagine the permutations.'

'I'd rather not. It sounds horrific.' Encouraged, he stretched towards her and whispered, 'Stella, let's hurry and finish all this and get home.'

'How can we, Michael? After today,' and leaned out of his embrace.

'Why not?' he insisted. Would it be so obscene? Whatever she might owe the dead it was not abstinence. 'Come on, don't weaken. You provoked it, with your Digby Doll.'

At which she sniggered.

'What are you giggling at?'

'Another aspect of laying the ghost.'

Chapter Seven

Miss Carey was small, dainty, with blonde hair combed into a circling bandeau, pink nails shining through transparent varnish, a way of sucking in her mouth to indicate emotion, and a fascinating wardrobe accumulated before clothes rationing which included a number of open-work jumpers pulled over her skirts and gathered in by black patent belts and showing, when stretched, modest lozenges of artificial silk – pink, blue, and on one occasion, black. She also had youth, an attribute inevitable in most lives but one she wore like an award for exceptional merit. Added to which, she had a boy friend.

'He joined up immediately after we had come down,' she explained, pulling in her top lip. 'We were engaged, of course, but not officially,' defending the absence of a ring which relegated her to the same shameful category as the majority of her colleagues. 'Then almost immediately after he had won his wings, he was shot down and taken prisoner. I live for his letters.'

Miss Carey's revelation occurred in the library backed by the shelf and a half of poetry beginning with Sidney's Apology for it. She generally flitted between there and the more expansive rows of novels whilst she indulged in chat, rarely moving to the half shelf of Criticism since it was the other side of the stack and exposed to draughts from the corridor outside. She was not in the least formal. When Stella had observed that one of the extra-curricular duties of the new mistress was the library and so had made herself indispensable there, her expectation had been nothing greater than humble proximity. Friendship, she often said to herself, had been beyond her wildest dreams.

'I've read nearly half of *Sense and Sensibility* already, Miss Carey,' she volunteered.

'Good. Read another of hers and then we'll start you on some of the eminent Victorians,' running her polished nails along their spines. 'It is essential to read widely, then gradually you will be able to discuss and argue. We would do that for hours, which was more valuable than a whole wilderness of lectures.'

Stella imagined the two heads bent over the open volume, the flames dancing light on the creamy page and upon the hair, pale gold, falling from a jewelled comb against the other, black and close-curled, while his left hand rested shyly on her nape. They looked up smilingly and began to talk.

'It is amazing how little time there is for reading later on. For example, there is something I have to attend tomorrow, and running the junior library after school means that I shall hardly have time to get back to the flat and smarten up.'

'There is no need for you to stay, Miss Carey. I'll do it.'

'Would you really? But it is not just tomorrow that is difficult. It is almost every Wednesday.'

'Oh, I'd love to do it! What is tomorrow's lecture about?' Resolving to read the relevant book that evening.

'Lecture? Oh, something on Jacobean drama, I think. Very learned,' and the woman went round to the draughty shelves to cool her blushes.

'And you mean to tell me,' Hubert exclaimed, 'that you

want to bike to Bingham every Wednesday morning and leave your bike behind the cobbler's so it's waiting for when you catch the half-past five bus that only goes as far as there? You'll not be in the house till near enough quarter to seven. You must like that library of yours. Do you think that's what you'll be wanting to take up, working in a library? You might as well; I'd have no objection. It's regular hours and a clean job. That is, if you keep to the outsides of the books.'

'Oh, Dad!' she reproached, amused, for his comment could be tolerated in the memory of Miss Carey's gratitude. 'I've no idea what I want to do yet, except go to university.'

'I know all that can be objected to in this,' Miss Carey stroked the tip of an index finger down the fold of a page, 'but I find it beautiful. So beautiful:

> "And after,
> Frost, with a gesture, stays the waves that dance
> And wandering loveliness. He leaves a white
> Unbroken glory, a gathered radiance,
> A width, a shining peace, under the night."'

The girl's eyes, too, began to water and though the airman she was thinking of had no similarity with a soldier dead of septicaemia in another war, he became invested with the poet's mantle. His black hair paled and shone as if spun out of sunlight and his face was transfigured with the beauty of sadness which, whilst contemplating death, could yet turn to welcome her smiling.

'It's funny to think of you leaving home. Had enough of your old dad, have you?'

It was hard to admit that the hand weighing upon hers was not white and manicured, but, 'Course not. Anyway, it's not for ages yet.'

'You've got something there. No sense werriting over what might never happen. Still, it's a facer. Think of it, if my girl went to Oxford and Cambridge!'

'I'm putting you in for open scholarships,' Miss Carey corroborated. Anticipating her consequent status in the staff room, she groomed her first candidate.

With an unselfconscious gesture, he lifted her hand to his lips before moving to the hearth rug and preparing to shave. As he bent down to fill the tin ladle from the boiler at one side of the range, she saw her reflection in the mirror above the mantelpiece, framed by the tea caddy and the clock holding back letters, then the matching wooden candlesticks ringed with his cycle clips and, on a shelf at one side, the *News of the World Dictionary* bought for her use leaning against the complete works of Longfellow, double columns of minuscule print and tissue pages to protect the sepia illustrations. While he squatted beneath, holding the brass handle of the tap with a handkerchief streaked with snuff; and his hair, thickened at the roots with the dust of plaster, neither shone in the dancing light of the flames nor was transformed by a discriminating alchemy into gold.

'I wonder whether I should apply to some of the others.'

Miss Carey raised her eyebrows.

'All over the place, are they?'

'Of course, the provincials are very sound,' Miss Carey admitted, 'but they cannot offer the atmosphere, that sense of belonging to a close-knit community.'

'Some of those places aren't bad,' he remarked when she had told him. 'Take Sheffield. I went there once with a bunch of lads from the Palais in a dancing competition. It was the Charleston, and I'm not kidding, they damned near wiped the floor with us, and we reckoned we was pretty hot stuff. I had to go home on the train with both my trouser legs slit to the knee. Still, the folks seemed friendly. I had a mate once came from there and he never had anything to say against it. Not that he mentioned it above a couple of times.'

Miss Carey was smiling indulgently. 'You think that Oxford may be too glamorous for you? I cannot imagine what sort of people you think go there. The Colleges are only interested in brains and are open to anyone who can give evidence of having them,' Miss Carey romanticized lavishly. 'It's an experience not to be missed. Read *Gaudy Night*.'

'I have,' the girl answered. Sadly she learnt that love cannot coax empathy.

'Is Sheffield or one of them others cheaper, then?' Stella could not smile with Miss Carey, not even behind her hand. 'I mean with you staying at school past twenty, somebody's got to fork out.'

'If I did well enough I should get a County scholarship. For wherever I went. Mother's gone into it.'

'Ay, you can rely on that.' He banged the ladle in the hearth, sprang up and stood with feet astride. 'In that case, you go for the best. And remember, nowt ever stopped anybody in our family from getting what they was after. I married your mother, didn't I? And she was a tough enough nut, believe me. And just remember, there aren't many youngsters about that have had the advantages you've had. Toys! Sometimes I used to think we could've opened our own toy shop, you had that many, and it was the same with books when you started wanting them, different to when I was a lad. My father wouldn't let a book into the house; once came up behind me quiet when I'd got my nose in one and slung it on the fire. Said I could wait till I was bringing in a man's wage before starting on anything fancy. Mind you, I didn't blame him; a working man's got other things to do than moping over books. But I didn't say no to you and you allus had plenty: Rupert and Enid Blyton and the *Daily Mail Annual* at Christmas.'

Miss Carey was openly laughing now.

'I can see you've still got a thought for your old dad left here, though.' His eyes had not left her face. 'I know what you're thinking. But don't fret. I'll still be here when you come back from wherever you are and we'll have some rare old times together.'

'There is no experience more valuable than mixing with your peers,' Miss Carey mused. 'Socially, of course, as well as academically, if one can make the distinction.'

Leaning against the cushions, they threaded deftly through ideas with easy ownership, their features repeating those of men who now commanded battalions. Receiving from her no answering memory of St Moritz before the war, they slanted away, leaving nothing to regard her but a face stale with dried sweat and shaded with a day's beard.

'It's not like my girl to be stumped like this,' it was encouraging her. 'When it comes to it, you might not want to go buggering off, leaving your dad on the end of the queue for kisses. I know what's bothering you. Cheer up! It may never happen.'

'I think it will.'

The ambiguity stiffened him like a cramp, circled his forehead and gripped the scarred socket round the enamelled shell. He jerked round, tore out the glass, dropped it in the egg-cup on the mantelpiece and ground his knuckles into the bone of his cheek. 'My God! This isn't half giving me some jip,' he groaned. Then, nursing the aching emptiness in a hand, he said to her, 'If that's what you want, then I hope you'll not be disappointed. I know nowt about it. When I was a lad school was filling in time before we could earn our keep and it felt like doing time, I can tell you. We didn't need to know no more'n what the teachers managed to shove into us, what bit that was, considering the work mapped out for us. Funny how we never gave that a thought; it was as certain as breathing. But it's not the same for you, Stella, and I'm pleased. I'll not stand in your way.'

Out of the corner of an eye she caught the flick of the other's sneer.

'It won't be *that* easy, even if you don't stand in my way.'

He flinched and his fingers clawed at the sunken lid.

'I mean, it won't be easy to get in, whatever encouragement you give me,' she gabbled. She wished she could faint or run away.

It was necessary for him to believe her. 'I see. And you'll get all the encouragement I can give you, all right.' Pushing himself away from the mantel, he turned to face her. 'When you go off to Oxford and Cambridge or some such place, schooling, I'll be thinking of my girl and keeping my fingers crossed that nothing crops up to stop her from what she's set on; and it'll mek no difference, her being a cut above her dad when she comes home, because she'll not alter her feelings. I know my girl.' In his face a lid flickered momentarily over the one eye regarding her, while from the raw hollow open before her a thin rheum oozed. 'Because we're as alike as two peas, her and me, and she was only happy being with her dad and she'd come running like a little terrier as soon as he'd set foot inside that door, jumping up and trying to stick her arms round his neck and nothing can ever put paid to that.'

Then his arms stirred at his sides.

She could not move towards him. 'I suppose not,' she answered miserably.

'That's all right, then; you're the one as should know.'

Bitter at being repulsed, he swung back to the fire, drained his blank with a finger and flicked the moisture

57

onto the coals before picking up the shirt which lay airing on top of the boiler.

'Why this bloody shirt's scorched!' he exclaimed savagely. 'Where's your mother? Alice!' he yelled. 'Alice!'

'Somebody's scorched this shirt at the neck,' he complained when she appeared. 'Look a treat in this, shan't I? It's about time people round here learnt to use a flat-iron.'

'It's hard not to make mistakes sometimes, especially when you've just taken the iron off the bars. Enid's usually a good ironer, but she was probably rushed. She's been doing extra jobs this week.'

'Then she shouldn't have been set on this. You can't blame her. She's got enough on her plate.'

'I'm not blaming her. She's a good girl and we work in very well together.' Their co-operation was a further irritant. 'I don't think it will show, Hubert. When you are wearing a collar it will cover most of the mark.'

'I'll go to blazes! So I've got to wear a collar now to cover up scorch marks! I suppose if the collar'ud got a mark I'd've been told to go around in a scarf! It's up to me to make the best of it. Well, I'm telling you it's not. It's your job to see as it doesn't happen – but not likely. You're too wrapped up in that school. The rest can go to pot, me included. It's allus the same with you people, so interested in schooling and books you've no thought for anything else.'

Alice looked at her daughter but her eyes were on the floor. She saw the fingers tight over the satchel and replied tiredly, 'It isn't often that anything goes wrong, Hubert.'

'More by luck than management. All I want is a clean shirt. I've said I'll be over at Bingham to fetch some eggs. Bloody marvellous, isn't it, having to go as far as Bingham before you can find a farmer willing to sell a few eggs. Of course, you won't ask here, we shouldn't have anything to do with the black market; but I know someone as doesn't mind: one of Stella's teachers. Keeps dropping hints. Knows what's good for her and not afraid of saying. Her and me would have a lot in common. But I shall look a proper bobby dazzler turning up in Bingham in that.'

'Put your best shirt on, then, and I'll get this out with cold water.'

'You needn't bother. My working shirt's good enough for any farmer. And I don't reckon I'll bother to shave, either. Nobody's concerned with what I look like. I'll get out as quick as I can; she'll want the table,' glancing significantly at Stella's satchel. 'At least I'm good enough for collecting eggs.' He turned back to the hearth, dismissing them both. Seeing himself in the mirror, he paused, then he smoothed his hair and reached towards the egg-cup. 'And I'll drop Enid off, if you can spare her. I've got a gallon in the tank, not the right colour, but it works just the same. I think she'd be glad of a ride on the pillion. We all have to find some way of enjoying oursens.' He smiled at his reflection, then lifted the ladle off the hob and went into the kitchen to shave.

'What a marvellous surprise!' Miss Carey peeped into the bag. 'It seems a lifetime since I saw a dozen eggs! It is most thoughtful of your father, Stella,' and carefully placed the bag on the table against two bound copies of *Punch*. Her appreciation clearly stopped short of payment. 'Is he in a reserved occupation?'

'Oh, no. He had an accident before war broke out. It blinded him in one eye so he was not called up. He threw some empty cartridge cases into the fire, only one was full and exploded. I don't know how it sort of worked because I wasn't there,' trying to give a complete explanation for a teacher, 'but Mum was, and she did try to save his eye only it was all slippery and hanging down his cheek . . .'

'I'm sure it must have been terrible,' Miss Carey

interrupted hastily. 'However, running a large estate now-adays is as important as being in the armed forces.'

'Dad isn't a farmer. He works on aerodromes, though by now he's finished laying runways.' She concluded apprehensively, but love demanded honesty, 'He was always in the building trade.'

'Really? How interesting!' The woman was looking at her in a new way, reassessing, adjusting, finding a new category. 'But I understand that your mother is a teacher.' She sucked in her lips, unable to think of anything to modify what the final comment betrayed.

'She is.'

Miss Carey was now thoroughly ill at ease. 'Well, she will have gone through college and training,' she stated, and this time the girl did not correct her assumption, 'so she will know what we are trying to do with you.'

Fifteen years later the woman could smile at that irony, but then she could make no objective judgement of Miss Carey. Standing with her dainty waist emphasized by stiff black patent, her instep arching prettily out of snakeskin court shoes, her azure eyes bravely concealing an inexpressible affection for an airman/poet locked in another land, Miss Carey was everything that the girl desired to be and, with the books of the school library at her shoulder and one pale hand leafing negligently through the pages of the *Illustrated London News*, she possessed the thing to which Stella now aspired: Culture.

'I can think of worse reasons for wanting to do well,' Michael had once commented. 'Desire for esteem is quite normal and fairly harmless.'

At the time she had been disturbed by that epithet. Now, arranging the buff envelopes and the small abandoned aeroplane brooch in the suitcase, its thought repetition whipped out at her, finding a raw place.

'Friday night and money burning holes in my pocket,' he called happily as he entered the kitchen. 'Except that I don't give it a chance.' He tore open his wage packet, withdrew a note and some silver and slid them under the clock for Alice. 'Why don't you come for a bike ride with your old dad and see what we can find? Make the place sizzle,' and laughed at the notion.

'I've an essay to write, Dad.'

'Well, do it tomorrow. What's it going to be about? Is it the same as what we used to call composition?'

The Sixth had read Browning's 'Up at a Villa, Down in the City' and Miss Carey, with the predictable ingenuity common to teachers of English, had made it the basis for a general essay: Discuss the view that town and country are not simply examples of two very different cultures but appeal to two fundamentally opposed facets of the human temperament.

'Well, I know where I'd rather be,' Hubert commented. 'Anybody who chooses to live in a hole like this wants his head examining. They did examine mine, years ago, and do you know what they found? Nothing. Scared them to death. If there had been, I'd never have come here, would I? It's got nothing, has it? There's allus something doing in a town – dancing, and shops, and your mates at work, and plenty of gossip, the sort they'll come right out with, not like here, standing glegging and saying nowt and spending twenty years chewing over whether they can open their mouths to say, How do.'

Disagreeing and repelled she did not answer; and she deliberately kept Browning from him. He was not to be allowed delight at,

"a mountain edge as bare as the creature's skull,
Save a mere shag of a bush with hardly a leaf to pull!

> – I scratch my own, sometimes, to see if the hair's
> turned wool.

'Come on, then, let's be having you. It won't take me long to get changed out of this. We'll bike over to the Fosse Arms. You can have a shandy in the kitchen while I see what's going on in the bar, then be home before dark.'

She was still smarting at his criticism of the country. Unlike him, she sought it, accompanied by poets whose descriptions gave precision to feelings and observation, whose lines she wept over with the sensibility of secrets shared. They were her mentors. They were Beauty and Culture and Miss Carey, who had surely rejected the urban shallowness of Browning and was expecting her to speak with their voice.

'I've got this essay to write, Dad.'

'Going for a bike ride'll get you in the mood, then.' He grinned and jangled the coins in his pocket. 'I'd like to treat you, though shandy's not much of a drink to treat a young woman to.'

'I don't think sitting in a pub kitchen is likely to get me in the mood for writing an essay.'

'Don't you look at me like that,' he flashed out. 'Lady Muck,' and saw the shock in her eyes and the gasping jerk of her head before he knew his hand jutting at his shoulder. Appalled, he pulled it back and watched her turn and pass through the door.

His flesh, getting to be a woman, once his girl to fondle and bath and carry on his arm.

> A little devil at times, though, and he'd given her a
> few spanks
> That had done more to him than some fights he
> could mention,
> Racing the bike after and crying hisself sick.

62

She'd got to be taught though he didn't want to do
    it.
But he couldn't touch her now; she was grown, a
    good looker,
Yet there was more than that in it and hard to lay
    name to.
Summat to do with the way she'd stood up.
He could see himself in her and that's what had
    stopped him.
Though that look was a facer, you couldn't help but
    admire it.
He'd allus fancied himself, so what else could you
    expect?
Took after her dad all right, old one-eyed Nelson,
Got his brains too, and they weren't no one else's,
And making good use of them with plenty of
    schooling,
More than her dad. More than her dad.

Crouched over the table he felt a touch on his arm and turned eagerly; and Alice understood that it was not she whom he had expected and saw the smile that was not meant for her leave his face.

'Are you all right, Hubert?' she asked, concealing her hurt.

''Course I am. It's this doesn't half give me some jip,' pointing to the empty socket. 'It's like a red-hot poker going straight through you.'

'I'll get you a couple of aspros when I've put these flowers in water,' but was stopped by his outstretched hand.

'You look after me nicely, Alice.' The inflection was not that of compliment but appeal as he rested his blind side against her breast.

Thus she was informed of a scene between them. 'Of course. Nearly as well as you look after me,' and wished she could curl in his lap as she had once done, believing herself at rest.

'You're right there,' he said quickly and, sliding his arms up her body, rose and hugged her to him. 'There's no one can say I need learning to do that. You get yourself togged up for a ride to the Fosse Arms. It'll do you good, the exercise, after being cooped up teaching village loonies all day.'

Held in her left hand, the cowslips brushed her thigh but their scent did not reach her as his embrace crushed her breasts and his teeth bruised her tongue. 'I can't. I must do the baking for the weekend. It's not exercise I want nowadays.'

'You tell me what you want and I'll get it. Anything you say. Anything under the sun. Haven't I allus seen to it you don't lack for nothing? You come on out with me and we'll have a good time.' He kept his mouth over her ear, feeling the flush spread along his groin.

'All right, if that's what you want, but it isn't easy making time now that Enid's left.'

'It never was.' He dropped his arms and took a step back. 'You was allus doing something more important. That bloody school! Gets more attention that I ever had. It's either you fiddling with summat for that school or her at her books. Mind you, I'm not blaming her – she wants to get on – but nobody else I know works for the boss after hours like you unless he's paid for it. Give a fair day's work for a fair day's pay is my motto and when you get home you've a right to expect a bit of a good time now and again.'

'I've said I'll come out,' was all she could answer.

'If it's like that, you needn't bother. I don't want anything on sufferance. You can find summat better to do than coming out with me, I've no doubt. I don't know why I bothered to ask.'

64

'Time was you didn't, when you had other fish to fry.' Anger spurted at his peevishness.

Completely unprepared, he stared back at her. 'What d'you mean?'

'I didn't mean anything. It was just something to say.' The flowers shielded her belly; her free hand was out behind her, groping for the door.

'Give me credit for a bit more than that! Come on, spit it out!'

'You used to like taking Enid out, that's all.'

'Enid? I took her home once or twice. Don't tell me you're trying to mek something of that.'

'She's having a baby, Hubert.' Repressed for so long, the fact soughed from her.

'The poor little devil. You'd have thought she'd have had enough sense to keep her skirts down.' Then, slowly, 'And you're telling me you think it's me the father, is that it?'

Seeing her shrink away from his menace, he laughed at the contrast between her and the other who had stood her ground even before the greater threat of his raised hand.

'That's what they're saying.'

'They want to keep their noses out of it and watch their mouths. That goes for you, too. You're as good as telling me you believe it, aren't you?'

'No. I don't know. I wish I'd never heard. It's that people are talking.' She backed to support herself against the door.

'Let them talk. They're never happy unless their tongues is wagging ninety to the dozen. I don't tek no notice of what folk round here say. I never have done and I'm not starting now.'

He had stepped forward and his face was so close that she almost choked on his breath. 'I know that. But it isn't so easy for me; and it's not right for them to be looking the

65

way they do. They whisper and look at me differently. It's wrong for them to be like that.'

'So they mustn't talk about teacher, is that it? Nobody's to say owt about teacher she might not like. That's naughty. They deserve the cane. They ought to be showing respect, touching their caps every verse end, not spreading talk. You think you're above that, don't you? Well let me tell you, you aren't; and I'll tell you something else.' His right hand was heavy on her shoulder, his left fist hooked on the collar of her blouse. 'I don't care a tinker's cuss. It don't matter a fart to me what they say, and having them all glegging at their gates isn't going to alter what I do or don't do, not by a long chalk is it.' Crushed between them, the cowslips were giving off a fragrance which pricked his nostrils like a sardonic comment.

His hand clawing down from her collar so that its seam scored red at her nape, he dug at the flowers between them and flung them across the floor, thundering, 'Get shut of these stinking things. They're enough to make anybody sick.'

Held up by his weight, she could only bend her head towards the splashed bells. 'What d'you want to do that for?' she asked, low and barren. 'One of the little ones picked them for me.'

At which, his muscles sank and his arms dropped from her. Stepping back, he watched her kneel over the flowers and saw her hair, light and soft as a child's, feather her cheek then cohere with wet. And he was down with her, down with one hand splayed over her spine and the other cupping her throat. 'I didn't mean anything,' he stammered. 'You're not to tek on about it. It made my blood boil, you saying that. You know there's nobody in the world means more to me than you.'

She nodded but continued to dabble her hands among

66

the bruised heads. These movements and her skin cold against his hand filmed his own with a clammy fear and he rose, not daring to be witness, and tearing his jacket from its hook in the kitchen fled from the house.

Where the twilight was thickening and darkness hung nets in the hedges and drew a false crust over the ditch; and only down the centre of the road was there a strip ambiguously lighter, known more by touch than by sight, for the air felt clearer there, still free of the scents which webbed it like rime above the grass. Until it, too, was sucked into the blackness under the hedge and he was left stripped of protecting light with the night hustling his flesh and nothing to companion him but the slight dilution of the darkness along the rim of the leaves. At the base of which a bulk shifted, its presence implied by the movement of denser black, then the swift hiss to a rustling dog. And this mass without feature or defined edge spoke to him, told him out of a mouth that he could not see to aim at that there was no use coming there, that she wasn't for the asking any longer and that he'd best be getting along. Which dragged him slithering upon the wrack of pebbles at the road's verge, stumbling over tufts, grappling with switching twigs and snaring briars, until he found a recess where space hinted a thing removed but rendered him nothing except a remaining draught. This piercing through his clothes hooked the impotent flesh like a barb. So for a time he floundered, tripped by taut roots, thrown over by the slime of discarded leaves, fingered by boughs, until finding the road again he tapped his way back along the gutters, his arms pushed out in front of him in a manner suggesting readiness to repel; or it could have been hope for embrace. For finding her alone, with glazed eyes staring into the fire and her body contracted to a thin curve against the back of her chair, he crouched and drew her to him, gasping out, on pinched breaths, his fear.

'You'll not hold it against me, will you? It's not true what they're saying, honest Injun it isn't. It's some other bugger that's done it, not me. All I ever did was take her home. I never touched her. You want to get her here and ask her straight. She'll not be able to say different. Except they're so ignorant she'll think me being like a father was enough. Someone must have done it to her since and she's too scared to say and lets folks think what they like. Don't you reckon her mam would've been round if it'd been me?

'Don't you believe them, duckie. I couldn't bear it if you did. You're the only one for me; allus have been. You know that.'

His face was upon hers and she could feel the cheek trembling. Habit informed present tenderness as she brought up a hand and stroked his hair, but the gesture was lifeless and the feel of him could give her no warmth. For the fabric she had built for herself was quivering, threatened by gazers, by the knowing looks of pupils alert to rumour, and a pervasive though reticent disrespect. So for the first time draughts not of her making had entered the classroom and, lacking anyone to shield her, she stood alone at her desk, hoping that soon these drear days would pass and that the sunlight slicing across her hands would once again have power to warm her flesh.

That struck him, too, with its coldness, and reaching up he took her hand and chafed it between his palms. 'You're all numb. We'll have to see what we can do about that. I don't know where you'd be without me to look after you.'

But that day she could not make the retort for which he waited. So, deprived, with a sense of being forsaken as never before, he sat and stared as she did into the coals.

While upstairs Stella, who had heard the shouts but not the words, sat with jaws clamped against the shaking and concluded for Miss Carey: It is certainly true that the country appeals to those whose temperament prefers solitude, such as Wordsworth. Though the contrast is greater in war time, the country has always been, as it is today, a place where one can escape from the cares and noise, where one can be alone and have time to think. One can also observe Nature, as W.H. Davies says,

"What is this life, if full of care,
We have no time to stand and stare?"
I like nothing better than to go for walks by myself, undisturbed by noise, when I can be happy or sad, without my feelings being affected by others.

Under this Miss Carey wrote, 'Rather thin and lacks vigour. Surely the country can be more exciting than this? The introduction of controversy would have given the essay more interest and weight.'

'Of course, she never would have believed it if anyone had attempted to describe that to her,' the girl, adult now, remarked to her husband. 'Miss Carey, I mean.'

'Pleased to have you back,' he greeted her. 'Still thinking about Miss Carey?'

'Yes. I've just realized that her idea of conflict was limited to tussles with the upper fourth and that if anyone had asked her if she had ever been affected by hostilities she would have sighed plaintively and gestured towards her fictitious airman.'

'Why so suddenly bitter about her?'

'Not bitter. Resentful.'

'This is new. You have always said how good she was.'

'I'm not questioning her scholastic ability. Do you think it would be a good idea to give Mrs Livesey this brooch?'

'I do, especially since he made it. I wonder what their relationship was? He always had plenty of libido and she is reasonably well preserved. Stop looking at me like that, darling. I'm a realist. Anyway, the brooch would be very suitable. Her period. Her war. Mine, too, for that matter.'

'And ours.'

'Oh, come on. What did any of you – or the village – know of the war?'

'It reached us all right. We weren't saved.'

'It seems I was lucky to pick up one of the survivors.' He was disposed to laugh, already planning how he would take her on their return. 'One so straight, firm and without a blemish.'

'You are deceived by the plastic surgery,' she answered him in a metaphor of his profession. 'Because when it came, it was ugly, violent, and flayed us all.'

Chapter Eight

She came a Fury, clawing out from the rubble wild and sharp as a broken nail, clattering down from the bus with heels snapping like castanets, rattling with the chipped and scorched flotsam from her wreck which hung upon her in slit carrier bags and one scored case with buckled lock, her scrawny body grating against the loathed, given clothes and strung taut over the child that remained; a woman spewed out of the dirt she had long before chosen, who glowered at the street she had once kicked behind her, a woman who returned neither prodigal nor fêted, thrusting before her the salvage of son and baggage, a woman who had not broken at impact but was kept alive by hate.

Thus armed, she parried the sympathy of the village, rebuffing hesitant condolences with granite stares until gradually this shy kindness withered and they comforted themselves with recollections they could then permit. For, a bastard by birth, she had spawned another before she left them, carrying it against her thin breasts to a city which absorbed her and asked no questions, but out of which occasionally news had crept darkly, tweaking the gossips with contradictions, stories of marriage and children, of lovers and lechers, of a home safe and cared for, of a life paced out brazenly along the dank alleys. So they gathered and considered, watching for signs that might betray her, while she beat the dust from her grandfather's rugs and pinned out decorous knickers donated by W.V.S. ladies. Spying, they expected a woman abandoned; lit by grief she would present a piquant vision of carnality and pain. But, hoping for thrills, they were disturbed by their nature. She was like a whip poised for scourging, looking about her with a dry, sexless anger, her eyes staring from ruin the watchers dare not imagine, pimpling their flesh with intimations of horror, at which they retreated as from one accursed. Therefore she was avoided, though she noticed that no more than their prying and, having arranged her wrack among that of her grandfather, she kept to herself.

But she did not grow tranquil. The fire that had been started in her would not burn out in solitude and the quiet ticking of the days. It was voracious and unappeased, demanding more prey upon which it could leap. Leaving her charred but at peace. No tinder came near her, however, which merited this fastidious fire until she was led to it by her son.

From the beginning, against the wall of the cottage, she had stood guard over his intercourse with the village boys. He was tall, well grown and had the quick wits which are trained on industrial streets. For which, together with his knowledge of the world, or so it seemed to them, and his urban poise which outstripped anything their fathers could command, the village lads gave him mocking but real respect. So he required no one's protection which his looks, though not his tongue, dared to indicate each time he joined her; but she continued to watch since all other things having been destroyed, the welfare of her son was the one constructive passion that remained. Which was licked by the flames within her one late afternoon when, shouting goodbyes as they went to their homes for tea, the boys called him: Side-arse.

'Why do they call you that?' she demanded as he entered.

'Just for something to say. It's their idea of a joke. You *know*, Mam; it's because of my name.'

'You're called Roe.'

'Well she put Sidebottom down on the register. Don't let it get you, Mam. It doesn't bother me. Anyway, a couple of names might come in useful sometime.' He leered out of a fantasy of necessary aliases.

'She'd no right putting Sidebottom in the register. Your name's Roe. She's like the rest of them, digging things up, allus ready to make you pay as if they were the parson, and no better than the next one, but lucky not to be caught out. I'll go and tell her and she can bleeding well change it. No, you needn't come,' staying his eagerness to witness a scene guaranteed to brighten the boredom of a village evening and, snatching her coat, slammed out of the house.

'I've come about about my Cliff,' she announced to Alice.

'Won't you come in? I've just put the steamer on the fire and I ought to keep an eye on it.'

'No, thank you, I'd rather not. It's he said you've put Sidebottom for him in the register, and I'd like you to know that's not his name. He's Roe, same as me, and if you don't believe me, take a look at this,' shaking her left hand in Alice's face so that she should appreciate the wedding ring. 'That proves it.'

Though unprepared for this outburst, Alice held to correct practice. 'But Cliff was born before you were married, so he has your maiden name, unless you changed it by deed poll, but you didn't mention that when you brought him in to school.'

'Deed poll be damned! He's called what I say,' she shrilled. 'Anyway, whatever you make out, you don't know so much because you've got it wrong. Cliff was my husband's.' The woman's face was sly, triumphant. 'The one I left here with, that everyone turned their noses up at because it hadn't got a father, he's gone. A bomb got him, buried him in the cellar alongside me and Cliff, which shows how much you know about it. Teachers! Think they know so much and they haven't the first idea. So I'll thank you to keep your nose out of my business and you make sure my Cliff is called proper or I'll be round again.'

Alice knew she was lying but argument was silenced before the reality of the legitimate son's death and, distressed by the woman's accusations and bitterness, she agreed to do as she wished.

'Amy Roe has been here complaining that I put her son down in the register as Cliff Sidebottom,' she told Hubert as he drew up to the meal. 'She wants him called by her married name.'

'What's wrong with that?'

'He's illegitimate. He should be entered exactly as he was baptized. That is what I have to do. That has always been the way.'

He shrugged. 'Seems a lot of fuss about nothing. Who cares what you put? You can carry on as you like. You don't have a boss breathing down your neck. You don't know when you're lucky.'

'If an inspector comes he always looks at the register very closely. It would be dreadful if there were anything wrong with it. But she was so nasty, the way she spoke to me.'

'What can you expect? You can tell what she is a mile off,' glancing quickly at Stella. 'She reminds me of a woman down our street at home. Scratch your eyes out as soon as look at you.'

'She lied to me. She said Cliff came from her marriage and it was the other son that was killed.'

'What did I tell you? Women like that – I've seed 'em – wouldn't touch them with a barge pole.' Then, because dishonesty was not the quality he referred to and which he had no instinct to condemn, 'She's got a cheek, I must say, but you have to give it to her. Fancy saying summat like that! Best one I've heard for weeks. You can see that she's not going to let owt get in the way of what she wants.'

'That doesn't excuse lying.'

'Not everyone can afford to be fancy.' Smarting at her rebuke, he jabbed his fork into his potatoes. 'These bloody spuds are burnt. It beats me how anyone can manage to burn spuds.'

'I'd just put them on when she came and a few at the side of the steamer next to the fire had caught before I could get back to it. I thought I had fished them all out. I'm sorry.'

'What's the use of being sorry? It shouldn't have happened. You can't even steam a pound of spuds nowadays without burning them.' Scooping up potatoes, he held them above his plate then let them drop back. Gravy splashed out. 'You'd be better occupied seeing to them than sitting judging who's telling fibs and what's to go in your register.'

Seeking distraction from the sprayed cloth, she took up his words as they came to her. 'I said I would change the register. It was beyond me to wrangle over her dead son.'

'I don't want to know any more about it, d'you hear? What goes on at that school is your worry and I tell you to keep me out of it. I don't care a shit in hell. When I come home from work I want the place tidy and summat decent to eat, not lousy potatoes so scorched and full of smoke you'd reckon they'd been in the blitz.'

He lifted his plate high above the table, then smashed it down. The food bounced up and fell back in glutinous radials over the crockery or was sucked into the stream of

75

gravy which oozed over the cloth between the halves of the broken plate.

'Leave it be!' he snarled, pushing Alice away. 'And what're you looking at?' he shouted at Stella. 'Why don't you bugger off and get on with that homework? But you needn't bother. I'm going. If I can't get anything to eat, I know where I can get a drink.'

Staying only to roll down his sleeves and collect his jacket, he strode out of the house; and though still raging as he pedalled his cycle out of the village he slowed down when he reached the woman's cottage. 'So you made her change her bleeding register,' he addressed her under his breath. 'There's not many as could. You must have summat. I mean, as well as what we know you've got. But you can keep that. I never had any truck with your sort. That way's dirty and when I have it, I want it clean.'

'You mustn't take too much notice of this,' Alice said, fighting to keep her hands steady as she cleared up the mess. 'When he flies into a temper it looks worse than it is. He's a good husband and father and would kill himself if anything happened to either of us. There are lots of women who would be glad to be married to him. It was my fault he did this, going on about the school. It irritates him. He likes to have a rest from anything to do with work when he gets home. I think this has got worse in the last year or two; perhaps it is something to do with the war, because he wasn't always like this. Oh, no, you mustn't think that. He was kind and gentle and used to help me with things at school, make little things I needed,' fantasy supplying what memory could not. 'I think you ought to go and do your homework now, dear,' unable any longer to suffer her daughter's face. 'I'd rather do this myself. I can manage. Please go.'

Left alone, she scraped up the food and china and

76

washed out the cloth whilst from the radio greater disasters slid over her mind and gave permission to tears; but these brought little relief and soon drained back, leaving her with lids blistered and eyes inflamed.

In which her school wavered, receded, then returned distorted, its walls leaning in upon her cracked by subsidence, and its splintered windows covering her with fractured light from a playground where the older boys gathered, winked at Cliff and sniggered at his stories and, taking their cue from him, did not file into their desks immediately at her bidding but stood about for a time before jostling in noisily, banging down their seats and staring with an awakened boldness at the girls.

Because the new boy had been infected by his mother's triumph, by her scorn for the teacher's tight-lipped rectitude and her resentment of this representative of authority standing unscathed; all of which pointed an aim for dissatisfactions and encouraged him to invigorate the tedium of this flat, low-pulsed living, void of the excitement of sirens and air raids and the morning truancy going unnoticed or kindly excused. Even so, he did nothing at first which Alice could not deal with. He was not vicious and was too lazy to sustain lengthy confrontation, relying upon indolent protest against what was required of him, on growled interruptions, on guarded mockery of children rewarded. This behaviour was irritating but during the first months spasmodic and she punished it by denying him playtime, so keeping him back in the classroom to be plagued by sounds of those free outside since the other boys, however impressed and admiring, preferred to observe rather than take part. Except for Desmond, Enid's youngest brother. Often associating himself with Cliff's conduct, he was willing to be confined with him, and when he was not, he would hang about the cloakroom or, apparently uninterested in fields, wait at the gate.

Where he was joined by Cliff's mother.

'What you been doing with my Cliff?' she shouted on the first occasion when he and Alice came out of the school. 'I'll thank you to send him home at the right time. There's his tea waiting.'

It was the first time Alice had ever been approached in this manner and though startled she locked the door and dropped the keys into her basket before walking slowly towards the woman. 'You wish to speak to me, Mrs Roe?' she asked quietly.

Infuriated by her calm, the woman bristled. 'No, I don't much want to. There's plenty of folk I'd rather be seen talking to but I've come about my boy so I can't be choosy. I'm asking why you kept him in.'

'He was rude and didn't do as he was told, so he had to do the work properly after school.'

'You've no right to keep him. You didn't think about me, I'll bet, not knowing whether he was all right. You're too concerned with getting your own back. If he doesn't get in when he's expected, how do I know what's happened to him?'

'There isn't very much that can happen to him here, Mrs Roe.'

'That's what you think! There are ways. And one is having a teacher that takes it out of him.'

'That isn't what I'm doing. If he is late again you will know why, so there will be no need for you to worry about him.'

Defeated by argument, the woman henceforth concentrated on abuse.

'I've told you to stop taking it out on my Cliff,' she would yell, drumming on the door of the cloakroom. 'What you locked this for, I'd like to know? Don't you think you can beat me, you mean stuck-up bugger. I'll have you reported, locking him in when he should be home. You don't know what it's like to be cooped up waiting. You're nowt but a walking machine with your ink and registers and keeping kids in if they dare to say boo to you, which they mustn't do to teacher – as dry as chalk and twice as nasty.'

Such raging was sensational to the watching children who, as time passed, would loiter on the grass outside the school. They would stand well away from the railing woman and her patient attendant as if, their emotions divided between horror and excitement, they attempted to shun what hypnotized them. When Alice appeared they dispersed guiltily but she could see that their attitude to her had altered. It contained a new tendency to assess her, an expectant observation and a hint of swagger. This discouraged her from assuming their support which, easily led, they would have given. So she made no move and though the girls showed their loyalty by quiet unsolicited jobs about the school and hurried away from Cliff's mother, the older boys continued as audience and, instead of running home when Cliff joined his mother and Desmond, followed them in a silent cluster up the street.

Inevitably they came to follow his example in the classroom. Bored with punishments that did not falter, he developed more sophisticated ways of causing disorder which were more difficult than open defiance for Alice to pin down: ink was mislaid just as it was needed; a key, in a great fuss of assistance, was bent in a lock thus preventing use of the contents of the cupboard until repair; boys carrying scuttles of coal would weaken inexplicably as they entered the classroom, tipping lumps and gritty dust on the path to the hearth; when milk was drunk in school because of rain, the cardboard caps in the necks of bottles would be pushed down too abruptly so that cream sprayed over companions and over seats and desks which, inadequately wiped, would gradually sour the room with their smell; and when opportunities for this kind of unruliness did not present themselves or imagination flagged, the older boys under Cliff's tutorage found difficulty in understanding her lessons, pressed her to explain again problems in arithmetic they had before conquered, clamoured sycophantically for help with compositions, and gaped in wonder at the stories she read to them.

Ostensibly unruffled as she scolded and punished, Alice felt her stomach tighten and her brain quiver. Once she would have met them with a blunt roughness which soon would have disarmed them. Now this manner failed her. Always she felt the spite of the frantic woman dart on Cliff's tongue and, worse, saw Enid's anguish clenched accusingly in her brother's face, and she was weakened by feelings of anxiety and shame. No longer secure in her public standing and harried by private distress, she became aware of the fragility of her influence. The ease which experience had brought her now had to be consciously exerted and she recognized that it had deteriorated into command, to be striven for and vigilantly maintained.

'You're looking a bit whacked,' Hubert said one evening as he watched her undressing. 'Hurry up and get in here. I know what'll be good for you.'

'I'm having a lot of trouble with the big boys, Hubert,' she burst out. 'They're upsetting everything. It takes me all my time to keep them under.'

Maudlin after an evening's drinking and with a hand warming upon the down at her nape, he was disposed to sympathy. 'All lads can be little blighters at times. I know I was. But I reckon you're a match for any lad round here. It'll come out in the wash, don't you fret.'

'It's been going on for ages now, one way or another. It

80

started soon after Amy Roe came back. Nothing I try works properly. I go from one day to the next.'

'What they need is a good tanning. That'ud learn them. You're too soft.'

'I can't do that, Hubert. I can't, and I don't think it's any good.'

'It didn't do me no harm. Kids expect it. They know where they are if some'un lays into them. Forget it now. I want a cuddle. Why do you think I shaved so particular?' Before he went out. 'You just give them what for, like I tell you. It beats me what you'd do without me behind you. It's a good job I married you, you daft ha'peth.'

She moved closer and as his flesh quickened he heard her murmur what he took for an endearment. 'What is it, lovie? Can anybody hear it?'

She was touched by his gentleness. 'I wish you were behind me, Hubert. I need someone. Sometimes I feel I can't go on much longer by myself.'

'What do you mean by that?' His hand fell heavy on her. 'Are you telling me I'm no good or summat? Is that it? As if I haven't allus stood by you whatever you've done!'

Tiredly she saw the folly of appealing to him and grimly, obstinately and in bleak loneliness she resolved that she would do so never again. 'Of course you've been a good husband. I'm not saying otherwise. It's just that . . . Well, you've always wanted me to feel looked after. I've grown to expect it. Perhaps you shouldn't expect other people to prop you up.'

It was tactful but too sombre and he caught the ambiguity of the 'you'. Panic numbed him like one left for dead who, waking on a dark glacial edge coffined in silence, strains for a sound or movement which brings rescue or the belief that sentient life remains. Its continuance was assured only by the touch of her neck which spread warmth through his palm

81

and as she twisted slightly to relieve herself of its weight he was suddenly frantic to keep its feel secure against the frost.

'Snap out of it, will you? Anybody'ud think, to hear you talk, I hadn't done right by you. I reckon it comes to summat when I'm expected to help you settle a bunch of kids who only need a taste of the belt to make them jump to it. And saying things like you can't go on much longer, you're talking out the back of your head. Where d'you think I'd be if you behave silly?' Then he saw her face reddening, the lips drawn back from teeth hissing out breath and, underneath, his white knuckles studding her throat. Leaping back, he knelt at the end of the bed and with his hand on the brass rail of the bedstead which did not cloud at his touch, he sobbed into the night.

'No! No! Take your hand away!' his daughter shouted in nightmare, and her husband, woken from erotic sleep, lifted the arm which had fallen across her neck.

'It's all right, love,' he murmured, dazed. 'There is nothing. You were having a bad dream.'

'Yes. About them. Of the time he tried to throttle her.'

'I thought so.' There had been a period when this memory had obsessed her and he had been unable even to stroke her throat.

'It was marked,' she whimpered. 'Three thick stripes which she hid with a scarf. But that slipped when that woman started to shout at her.'

'Yes. Don't go over it again. Let me love you.'

'He had gone to that woman, had sex with her, and then returned and attacked the wife he had been unfaithful to, and the woman he had been with hung on her, bloated by the sight of what he had done.'

'You may be wrong, darling. You can't be sure that he ever had it off with her; and even if he had, you don't know when.' He pushed an arm under her, offering his warmth.

'It happened and the woman gloated over her. How could he do that to someone he was supposed to love?' Abruptly she pulled herself away from his embrace.

Rejected, he lay on his side, his arm outstretched against the headboard, still hoping she would turn to him. But how could he vanquish her ghosts? His touch had no substance against their warring power. 'I think he did love her, but not in the way we know.'

'How can he have loved her? He gave her nothing.'

'I don't think you can judge that.' Regarding her as she lay stiff on her side of the bed, he asked sharply, 'If you consider giving so important, how do you quantify your own?'

'What do you mean?'

'Sometimes, Stella, particularly on these occasions, I wonder how much you give. Perhaps I get what I deserve, I don't know, but that doesn't make it any easier.'

'I don't know what you're talking about. We have always shared everything. We have given equally.'

'No, Stella. I'm not talking about a bag of goodies. To be exact, it's not a question of giving but of giving up. That's the test. You tell me a great deal about your parents. I listen. I'm concerned. Your feelings about it all concern me. But you still don't tell me all. You keep some things to yourself. Those two are a barrier between us. You nurture them. You won't give them up to me. Sometimes I think you hardly need me at all.'

'Michael!'

'I mean it.' He was irritated that, in expressing injustice, he sounded like a child threatening the sulks. But he persisted. 'You make me a cuckold. With their ghosts. Why can't you just be straightforwardly unfaithful? At least, that way, there'd be rules to the game.'

'Unfaithful?' she repeated, bewildered. 'To you?' His

complaint had not reached her, only his tone, yet she tried to attend to him. 'Rules?' while the ghosts that had stalked through her sleep remained fretful. 'For them, there were no rules. It was so public. Terrible for Mother.

'That woman approached her in the middle of the street and struck at everything that was hers, exposed her, herself, her teaching, her marriage, to the gapes of people rushing to their doors, to the boys crowded against the pub wall, to the passengers in the bus not ten yards away, to me who had just climbed down from it and didn't know how to push past them all and get home. She was shouting at Mother that she didn't know how to run her school, that all she could think of was keeping kids in, and she called Mother a prude for punishing Cliff for some word he had written on the lavatory door, while he and Desmond sniggered and eyed the onlookers in a smug way. She said that Mother had done this in order to be spiteful to her, to show what sort of woman Mother thought she was, though other folks's kids could say it and not get it in the neck for it; but it was always the same, people were always ready to drag up what pleased them. Then she glared at everybody watching and they all looked away and two or three pretended to move as if they might be returning to their houses, but they didn't. I'm sure they didn't approve of her then, but none of them dared to intervene. They were too cowed by her tongue and afraid of what she might say to them if she turned on them instead. Then she swung back on Mother and called her a hypocrite. The word was shrill and loud and whipped round the people there who rustled as it passed over them, and Mother drew herself straight and tried to walk on but the woman grabbed her basket and held her back. "You're a hypocrite," she yelled, "telling our Cliff that's dirty and he ought to be ashamed of hisself.

Well, mebbe it is, but you're not the one to say. Because there's some folk don't stop at talk, isn't there? You've no call to go round being so high and mighty as if dirt'ud blush as soon as look at you, when there's them next to you won't bear examination. What about your old man? From what I've heard tell, he's not so shy about going a bit further than words, getting young girls in the family way and in your own house, too, which for the cheek of it takes some beating."

'It made me feel dizzy and I remember holding my satchel up in front of me like a shield and my ruler protruding from one of the burst corners and digging into my side. I wanted to run away, but I couldn't because I seemed to be surrounded by faces, some of them watching me but most of them fixed on Mother. They had changed. Before, I'm sure they had been disgusted by the woman; now it was as if a thrill had gone through them, that they felt a kind of satisfaction that someone whom they had always looked up to was being brought down, and their feet shuffled and they rested their arms along the tops of their gates and leant forward, waiting for more. I realized then that what she had said about Dad they believed and she was offering revenge. And it didn't matter if this were not received by the one they considered guilty; in fact it was safer to strike at the guiltless. It could have been me. It should have been me! It should! I wanted to shout out that they were wrong, that Dad had done no such thing, that nothing she said was true, but sick gushed into my mouth and I was swallowing it back because I couldn't vomit it out there at the bottom of the bus steps in front of them all. Through this I saw Mother look round then say something to the woman and again try to walk away, but the woman still held her basket. Tugged between them, it tilted to one side and her books and a loaf and the bacon she had bought on the way home for tea spilled over

85

the pavement and the bunch of keys for the school rattled out and fell in a stiff fan near the woman's feet. Nobody spoke. Mother gave a little cry when it happened and the woman made a harsh sound and kicked the keys away. Nobody moved. Mother stood holding the empty basket, her things scattered on the ground, and I did not run to help her. I couldn't. I was too frightened. I could not walk forward in front of everyone there and show that I belonged. I tried. I think I made a step. I shall never stop hoping that I made that step. Finally Mother crouched down, collected the things and placed them in the basket. In so doing the scarf slipped down her throat.

'It is possible that no one would have noticed, but the woman was near her and interpreted rightly what she saw. "So he's been laying his hands on you, has he?" and began to laugh. "Were you trying to keep him in 'cos he'd said summat dirty or did you say naughty boy for having a bit of skirt? I can't see him getting much at home. You can't keep him in order then, is that it? Beneath you, I suppose, to give him a taste of his own medicine. I haven't noticed him going around looking as if he'd been punched up. My God, you make me spit. I'd like to see the man who'd try anything like that on me. It wouldn't be me ending up like that, I'm telling you. He'd get a sight more than he bargained for, I'm not kidding!"

'When I got into the house, Mother had the contents of her basket spread on the table and was smoothing the crumpled pages of an exercise book. The scarf was tied in a pretty, floppy bow under her chin.

'"Goodness me," she greeted. "You here already! I didn't see the bus pass. It's later than I imagined." Her eyes held mine, willing me not to cry, and preventing admission of what we both knew. "I must hurry up with the tea," taking the bacon out of its split paper and wiping it clean of grit.

"This fell out of my basket but I don't think anyone will know that after I have washed it. If you don't mind, I should like you to start your homework straight away because there are several jobs I'd like you to do for me after tea. I've decided to have an early night. I've been feeling rather tired today."

'I left her and went up to my bedroom and sobbed my way through a Latin prose not only because of what I had witnessed but because so little had been exacted for my cowardice. Later, when Dad had gone out and she was washing before going to bed, she allowed herself an oblique reference to what I had heard.

'"I suppose you've heard that Enid's just had a baby. I feel very upset for her. She was such a nice girl. When I heard at first that she was expecting, it passed through my mind that she had left us because she knew and of course was far too shy and embarrassed to tell me; but it can't have been that, because if you reckon it up you'll see that it must have happened after she left us and went to Marshall's. Soon after, I suppose, but still not the reason for her finishing here."'

Chapter Nine

Now as Alice walked to school she was no longer serene, planning her day, but apprehensive, bracing herself for what it might bring. Yet she remained the teacher acknowledged by those she met. A man raised his cap, a woman beating carpets paused and looked at her through the dust, the veteran sentinel moved from her path; but the man's gesture was a little perfunctory, the woman's pause was shorter and followed by sudden busyness and the old man's shuffle was more effortful and slow. By such dilution in their greeting Alice understood that their habitual recognition of her calling had been modified by the mockery of the woman, and though still not hostile they had withdrawn, waiting to see what she would do. Now passing between the rows of cottages, down the private path by tradition permitted to the teacher, Alice no longer smelt the border of phlox and the laundered scent of clothes on the clipped hawthorn, nor observed with pleasure how her shadow rippled purple over lettuces and banks of potatoes; her senses were shrunken to flinched sight which expected the flick of a curtain, an arrested movement in a doorway, and to worried hearing as she strained for sounds of the early children.

This sniggering and nudging and huddling in corners is usual, the boys always do it as they approach fourteen, she reminded herself. It is only natural and it is bound to be vulgar – they are only repeating what they have heard. If he were not with the others and protected by distance, there isn't one of them would dare to shout anything to a girl. Made to sit next to one, particularly one who is more developed, every boy would be red with embarrassment and screw himself round on the seat to keep his back to her. We always have this some time before they leave school. I do wish we didn't because I find it annoying and after a time even the nicest girls are affected and giggle, as bad as the forward ones who, I suspect, in some way start the boys off; but they are careful that I don't see. We all have to put up with it, including the babies. Nothing I say has much effect when they are like this. It will pass. It is no different from what I've dealt with before.

But she knew she deceived herself. Because, before, there had been no Cliff.

For he had the precocity that towns foster, had observed shrewdly some of the war-time laxity and had novel stories to quicken their halting fantasies; and having witnessed his mother's outrage upon their teacher and their parents' craven acquiescence, they were freed from the restraints of village secrecy and Alice saw them as if possessed by prurience. It gave to their walk an unexampled vigour, lifting their feet purposefully in boots that had before slithered, pulling back shoulders that previously had rounded, thrusting out hips that once had sagged slackly, giving gestures to hands that had always hung awkward, pinking their skin over veins webbed coarsely and animating faces that had been often torpid but never lewd.

These she would outstare and with effort hide her disgust as she called the boys in to lessons; but when they were Desmond's eyes that preyed upon her she felt herself defenceless – in a place where there had once been neither

89

battle nor enmity – held up solely by the barren need to repress. For which reason she neglected those who were loyal to her or, thinking some remark or gesture had indecent intention, would turn upon them and see in their hurt and confusion and the tears of the babies the crumbling of their goodwill. So the old kindliness was lost, the forbearing community of an all-age classroom vanished, and she moaned as it split in her hands whose only cure now was desperate severity.

'Come out to the front, Holt,' she commanded. 'What's that you are playing with in your pocket?'

Supported by sniggering appreciation, indeed the very recognition of his presence, usually avoided, the boy slid out of his seat and shuffled up to her desk where, crushed between their laughter and her frown, his momentary courage left him and he began to snivel.

'Stop that,' she ordered. 'Let me see what it is.'

Timorously, with hand shaking, he brought out a little clutch of pebbles and laid them in the channel scooped out for pens. Behind him necks craned to see what he had produced. Small and undistinguished they stayed close together, slimed by the mucus which, hanging always at his nose, seemed to cover the rest of his skin like a frothed sweat.

'Don't pretend that's all. Hurry up. We haven't all day.'

He shook his head and his nostrils bubbled. A thin phlegm gathered along the weak gutters of his lower lids.

Alice looked at him with distaste she had once been able to control. Stupid and simple he was the youthful caricature of parents who astonished by their ability to survive the hardships of being practically unemployable and the demands of day-to-day living for which a dazed ineptitude was their sole equipment. He was the first of the family scattered across the desks, all of them cocooned in a private world of blurred impressions and having no distinction from one another except the inchings of stunted growth. She could give scant time to them and they sat through her lessons in trusting incomprehension, damply grateful for the moments of her personal attention. These cost her little patience; what did were the physical frailties of these children, the most important being incontinence when they were suddenly itched by emotion or stress.

Under her gaze the boy's nose dribbled. He rubbed his knuckles across his lip, drawing out the mucus over his cheek. Behind him the noise was no longer indulgent and he sensed that Alice's protection was withheld. A tremor passed through him and his pelvis began to move rhythmically in the slack greased trousers.

Alice knew the danger but she was angry at having exposed herself to ridicule. The challenge had been unnecessary, the victim guiltless and the booty contemptible.

'Are you telling me that is all you have in your pocket?' she insisted.

He nodded. Set in the groove of her desk, the miserable stones accused her. His body was jerking now, urgent and desperate. At sight of which her own was clammy, her hands glutinous upon the polished wood, while scoffing coiled round her and the rocking boy. Until the pallid face split open, a tongue burst out in horror and appeal, and 'Get to the lavatory,' Alice shouted.

He stumbled moaning out of the door but the mockery from which he fled remained to taunt her as, gathering up his pebbles, she found them stuck to her palm and she could not tell whether their viscid surface was from his exuding or her own. Punished by a final swish of amusement, she took the duster and wiped it over her hand.

'Have you thought what you might do when you have finished university?' she asked Stella. The months were

91

passing but for her each one promised nothing but dreary repetition of itself.

'Heavens, Mother! I haven't started yet. Four more weeks. Finishing there is the last thing I'm thinking about at the moment.' She was glowing, decked with success. The three years ahead were sunlit and stretched as limitless and unwithering as life.

Alice nodded but the pleasure she felt as she looked at her daughter was faded by weariness. Her strongest feeling was relief that the girl was going free. 'Of course it is, and I know you'll enjoy it. You deserve to, anyway.' Out of the corner of her eye she saw Hubert stir and run a finger over the sunken lid. 'All the same, it is no bad thing to consider what you might do afterwards.'

Once she, too, had imagined no further than her daughter's goal. Now it seemed necessary to secure her future, like one anxious to bequeath what she cannot herself enjoy.

'That's ages and ages away, Mother. I just can't think of it. Honestly, bothering about things like earning a living! It's so . . . sordid!'

'It'll be more sordid if you don't,' Hubert intervened. 'Anyway, I don't know what you're fussing about,' to Alice. 'You know very well she'll be a teacher. It's what you've wanted all along. You've been angling for it for years.'

'There are other jobs,' she answered quietly.

'Not many I know of that can hold a candle up to yours. It's steady; the money comes in regular; there's the holidays. Mind you, there aren't many perks,' thinking of the materials from building sites which furnished his work bench. 'All the same, you're your own boss. Wish I could say as much,' he pretended, for he demonstrated independence by circumspect contempt for authority rather than by any aspiration towards it. 'You've no worries; nobody interfering with you.'

'That's not always an advantage.'

'What d'you mean? Some folks don't know when they're lucky. You're not telling me you want some'un else poking his nose in.'

'There are times when I'd welcome some advice.'

'You, advice? I'd like to meet the chap who could give you advice. After all these years! We'll have come to a pretty pass when you go round asking folks to tell you how to do your job.'

For a moment this expression of his old admiration for her was comforting, then the sweetness passed away. Reality could not sustain it. And his words were too facile, informed by necessity for himself, bludgeoning her to acquiescence in her part, forcing her to remain undiminished, the cast for his alloy. One which he reserved the right to condemn.

'I suppose I really mean that I should like to have someone I could talk things over with occasionally. Just little things that are always cropping up. It would be nice to have an assistant. Anyway, it isn't me we are talking about but Stella,' she tried to be brisk, 'and if she did go into teaching it wouldn't be in this sort of school.'

'I'm not going to teachers' training college,' the girl pointed out to him. 'With a degree you specialize, if you teach at all.'

'Are you telling me you go to university for three years and when you finish all you are fit for is teaching one thing?'

'You have to have a degree before you can teach any subject properly.'

'Some people manage to. Alice here never even went to college and she does the lot.'

'Of course. She has to. I'm talking about high schools. You know very well what I mean. It's not simply the three

R's, plus a few other things like how King Alfred burnt the cakes and what is the longest river in the world and what pretty patterns you can make with a pair of compasses and how much change you can get from half a crown for one and three-quarter dozen penny ha'penny stamps.'

'You'll do well if you get owt,' he grinned, enjoying her spirit, and straightening, patted the hair at his temples.

Which movement made her aware of her mother's stillness.

'It's just as well that I wouldn't have to teach everything if I went into teaching. I'm not versatile enough,' the girl tried to apologize.

'You manage,' Alice answered without expression.

Versatile. That's one word for it: making up the register; ordering coal; selling saving stamps; filling the lamp when the caretaker has forgotten; rinsing out a baby's knickers; drying clothes in winter over the fire-guard; bandaging hurt knees; ordering library books and pointing out their titles to women stooping over the shallow wooden boxes stored in the cloakroom. Stop that bullying! Playing the hymns; throwing bean bags. Will you please be quiet! Threading the sewing machine; gripping the whistle in my teeth as they all lumber through races. Be quiet! If you can't be more quiet then you must sit in silence. Examining heads for nits; cuddling a shy baby; helping a girl in the lavatory when she has just started; prising a mouse from the trap, its back broken and eyes cindery, my hands rashed by the prick of its fur where the dribble from the snout has set like a brown scab.

Her mother's shuttered life nudging the other out of her own just enough for her to be grazed with alarm, she continued, 'Well, honestly, I don't know how you do it. I mean, having to take every subject! It must be awful when you think of it, being required to talk on everything on the timetable from simultaneous equations to blank verse.' In her need to compensate she ignored fact. 'And it's not only knowing it but having the imagination to present it. History is easy, but think of geography. Thank goodness I dropped it after School Cert. I suppose you could start with the seasons which they can see out of the window,' she instructed her mother, 'but after that, I don't know. Perhaps you have to travel or something to make it really *live*.'

The Eskimos live in houses made of snow. They cut blocks out of the hard, packed snow, like bricks, and build little round houses with a hole in the middle of the roof to let out the smoke from the fire. Does the fire melt the snow? Oh, no, because the snow bricks are so thick and hard. Isn't it cold inside? Oh, no, because the snow keeps them warm. Their houses are very warm. I know because I have been there and stayed in one, right through their long winter when there is no sun and the days are dark as night. What did you say the Eskimo husband does, Desmond? Really? I do not know where your father got that from. My Eskimo host did not make such an offer to me. Yes, perhaps it was because I am a woman. No, I would not have minded at all if he had suggested that (laughter) because he was a very gentle, friendly man with warm fur trousers and jacket and hood and I am sure it would have been very nice to be covered up by all that soft fur until the days got light again and the sun warmed you and everything was as it had been before. And now we are going to make a model of an Eskimo village but since we have not any hard snow for making bricks we must build the houses out of plasticine, then we will stick cottonwool for snow all over them and you can make lots of plasticine figures which will not look as nice as my Eskimo host covered with fur but we shall have to pretend. We cannot always have things just as we would wish.

'There are not many that have done much of what by rights you could call travel, recently,' Hubert pointed out. 'Not and come back to tell the tale.'

'Of course I shall travel eventually, but if I ever went into teaching, as I've told you, I shouldn't be teaching geography – I don't know what I want to do – that is not the point of going up. You go for the subject itself and all that collegiate life has to offer,' the spires stabbing the scarfing clouds, 'not just for facts, but for knowledge, experience, don't you, Mother?' She was appealing to Alice to break her silence.

'That's right.' The woman dragged herself to give help where it was demanded.

'I mean,' the younger insisted, 'that education is more than having lessons after the Gradgrind fashion. By studying a subject thoroughly, especially on the Arts side, you come in contact with ideas and theories that in a subtle way mature your outlook on life.'

Your outlook on life. I don't think I've got one. Unless God is an outlook, but Stella doesn't mean Him and I can't say I ever thought of Him like that, not thought of Him at all, for years now, just said His name at school prayers. I've never had time for an outlook on life. Had to get on with it, doing the best I could, without many ideas or theories. I'm not so sure, either, they would have been much good. When he flies into a temper and smashes a mirror it doesn't much matter how I look at it; it's still me sweeping up the pieces, holding the tears back, as he bangs out of the house. It wasn't always like that so perhaps I might have stopped it, but things get going sometimes before you notice or really say to yourself that they are happening. And you don't always have the chance to work it out in time. When you're in the thick of it you don't get round to having an outlook. It was always the same: jobs for Mother, cramming

96

for exams, then looking after Hubert, and her, too, when she came along, as well as the teaching. Teaching the same as I'd been taught. It seemed the right thing. Maybe that's what she means by the Gradgrind method; I've never heard of it, but when you think about it, there isn't a lot of point – chanting times tables, dates in history, most of it forgotten as soon as they leave school. Though it's got to be got through. You can feel hemmed in by it. I didn't once upon a time, but I have done lately. Would it have been any better if I could have got outside of it? Would it have meant that woman would not have set Cliff on? If I had had the sort of advantage that Stella describes, would it have made any difference? Funny how I've never thought like that before; what I'd had seemed good enough. But when you're in the thick of it you have your work cut out just bearing it, so you have to make do without thoughts and theories. I'm not complaining. When you get down to it, one way or another we all have to make do.

'I'm pleased you are going to have the chance of studying ideas and theories,' she answered her daughter wanly but without bitterness. 'I'm sure they will help you to form a clear outlook on life.'

'Theories are for folks who don't know owt about life,' Hubert commented. 'You have to get out into the world before you can have an outlook.'

His own was bent upon himself, stopped by the barrier of the dark segment, so he paid heed only to the overt content of their exchanges. By these, as they felt their way through the blank side of his vision, he saw himself excluded. Saying nothing, sullen and resentful, he took his jacket and left the house.

Inside the pub there was noise and the atmosphere of companionship. Men nodded to him as he entered; the landlord said good evening; a pint was drawn for him and change given courteously. But the nods and the greeting lacked heartiness; the beer was served too promptly, and since no space was made for him at the bar he had to turn to a table where he sat alone.

Gloomily he wondered why he had come there. It was not his usual place. He was not one of the regulars, nor had he any other ties which would have secured him a welcome. Always he cycled out of the village, when he could not wangle any petrol, to a pub on the main road to the town. There the men were liberal, their money flowed easily. Coming out to a smart country pub to enjoy their earnings, they were a cut above the men he worked with and the men he had boozed with before he was married, but still town bred, recalling in their walk the sway of the dance halls, the promise of cinemas, the knowledge of park bushes, which was the closest to vegetation they ever wished to get. And when they were dressed in the uniforms of the services they were no different; they were still intelligible, still framed by the streets they had once lived in, still shouting above the clash of trams, whistling at corners, tripping over news stands, running for bookies. As he had once done. And he would be like them now, except a bit older, if it wasn't for this eye.

You're lucky, I tell you, wearing that uniform. Landlord, a pint here for the corporal. My God, what I'd give to be let join up! But once I'd got this (pointing) they wouldn't have me. Though I bet I can see more with one than most buggers can with them both. You think I'm barmy? You'd rather be in my shoes? That's some bloody way to talk, I must say. It's disgusting. And you with a couple of stripes on your arm. You ought to be shot.

On that occasion challenges were exchanged and Hubert laid out the corporal on the lawn behind the pub with three swift but not altogether legitimate punches; and as he rode home, tacking across the lanes like a schoolboy, he felt as if he had won the war single handed, the humiliation he usually suffered being on that night sloughed off. But he could not do that with the civilian clothes that caused it. In the company of men honoured by uniforms, his clothes hung on him like garments of disgrace and though most servicemen in that smart pub knew the smells of cities, had walked under street lamps, he was not their equal.

But here in the village he was more than that. There was no one here he had to look up to. There was no one here that'ud dare take him on. About as slow with their fists as they were in the head; you could tell them anything – not that he often bothered – their eyes poking out like cows' and nearly as stupid. They were watching him now when they thought he wasn't looking. Think because he had a pot one he couldn't see owt. They could think what they liked, and say, for all he cared. He knew what they'd be on about as soon as he left. They couldn't prove nothing. There was nothing to prove. He knew more about that than all the lot of them put together. He'd like to tell them a thing or two some time, see them slaver and their eyes pop out a treat. But it'ud not be worth it. Plodding behind horses' arses and pinching cows' udders, they thought it was no different. A waste of time, telling them owt else. So they could look at him sideways if that gave them pleasure, and though them at the dart board needed a new player – old Barnes dropping out wasn't much cop – they'd have to ask him. He wasn't offering. They'd think he was busting hissen for a game. He wouldn't have to borrow the pub arrers, neither. Always carried his own.

Getting up from the table he ordered another pint, the men at the bar making room for him while he waited but suspending their talk. Returned to his former place, over his raised glass he saw that the space he had left was now taken by a woman, the woman who had made Alice change her register. Grinning at the memory he kept his face half turned and regarded her over the bridge of his nose along the perimeter of his blindness. She had stopped talk more completely than he had, for the men at the dart board and those stooped over dominoes were as silent as the drinkers at the bar as she waited for the landlord to approach her, and her request for two bottles of Guinness came loud, defying the stillness. She knows her way about, he said to himself; only her sort would come in here by herself. Yet the woman's manner did not solicit. She glowered round the watching assembly, chose a victim and stared him out before examining her change. This she did under the eye of the landlord with obvious suspicion, then, tightening the strings of her overall, a stained covering which would not necessarily have discouraged advances in that unfastidious company but which she bore like chain mail, she gripped the bottles to her breast. When she had gone the gap at the bar closed again, the talk burst loud, but no one called to Hubert and asked his opinion, and with the sense that her isolation had confirmed his own he quickly drained his glass and left the pub.

He did not examine the impulse which made him follow her, only attentive to the hunting craft which kept him well behind until, overtaking her as she neared the cottage, he stopped as if noticing her burden, stepped back and pushed open the gate.

'Mustn't have an accident with those,' he said, indicating the bottles.

'I can manage.' She did not thank him and latched the gate between them.

'Looks as if you're set on enjoying yoursen.'

'It'ud take more than two bottles of Guinness. They're for him,' nodding over her shoulder.

He had forgotten her grandfather. 'He does all right, then, doesn't he? Having some'un to fetch for him.'

'He's nobody else. It doesn't cost me no bother.' Uninfluenced by any desire or nicety of obligation to converse, she was turning up the path. Perversely Hubert wished to delay her.

'I haven't seen you in The White Hart before,' he said more loudly.

'I haven't seen you for that matter,' she retorted. The faint challenge in his tone had halted her. 'But I seen you tonight. With a face like a wet week. Looks as if you might as well save your money, or try summat stronger.'

'I wouldn't mind that, in the right company.' He was startled to hear the invitation.

Which she ignored. 'If you don't like it there you should go somewhere else.'

'I do as a rule. I've never had much time for them round here. They're a tight lot, and bloody ignorant. Some of them haven't even got the wireless. Getting them to talk is like squeezing blood out of a stone. Not the same as the folks back home.' He spoke as if an ocean not twelve miles separated him from his birth place.

'You don't have to tell me. D'you suppose I'd have come back if it hadn't been for that ruddy bomb?'

For a few moments they stood in silence for her son. Then he said plaintively, 'There's not a deal goes on. You can get sick for company.'

'Tell that to the Marines. You have to learn to do without. There's your missis.' She gave a sudden, harsh laugh. ''Course, you don't want that. I know what goes on there. I've seen your marks on her.'

He was shocked by her knowledge. 'It was an accident,' choking on the memory.

'Some accident! You must think I'm crackers. I've got

nowt to say for her. You can put her out cold for all I care. But, by God, if I was in her place you wouldn't get off so light. No one lays a finger on me and gets away with it. Coming in boozed up and starting a rough house! I wouldn't stand for that. You'd bloody well take me with you and come back sober, or carry your drink without getting nasty.'

He had been astonished and repelled by her hatred for Alice, squaring himself up ready to defend her, but as the woman's vehemence ran on he was provoked in a different manner and he felt his flesh tingle.

'I can just see you putting up a good fight,' he answered and his voice was warm, admiring. 'You'd make a good sparring partner.'

In the darkness the woman stirred and the bottles came together in a low muted note. 'Don't you kid yourself. I don't get mixed up in fights for the love of it. You'd best find some'un as does. I'm going in. The old man'll be wanting his drink.'

He smiled at her offering a reason.

'Ay, he'll have worked up a regular thirst by now. I'll have to drop in and say how do to him some time when I'm passing.'

'Please yoursen. He hasn't got much to say for hissen nowadays.'

She was moving away. 'Reckon he hasn't much of a chance with you about,' he laughed to stay her but she made no answer.

'I'll be round then, one of these days.'

'Do as you like,' she repeated. 'It's not something I'll be banking on.'

A compact made.

Chapter Ten

'She seems just the same as ever, doesn't she?' Hubert commented. The letter was propped up against his cup. 'Having a good time, too, by all accounts, not that I blame her, but I hope she doesn't forget what she's there for.'

'I don't think she will.'

'Didn't have much to say at Christmas, what bit I saw of her, but she don't stint herself when it comes to putting it on paper. That way, of course, she doesn't give us the chance to ask questions. She's a clever 'un. Like her dad.'

She's got his brains all right,
And had plenty of schooling.
More than her dad.

'You could always write to her, ask her questions if you wanted.'

'That's your job. I'm not one for writing letters. What do you make of this bit? Dancing. "Afterwards there were not enough bicycles to go round and some of the men had to walk three miles home."'

'After the dance.'

'I know that! It's these men I can't make out. Locals, I suppose.'

'I should think they are more likely to be undergraduates.'

'Well, I reckon that's a crying scandal. It shouldn't be allowed. Sitting there on their backsides when they should be out there with the lads. It's not over yet by a long chalk.'

'I suppose they are exempt for some reason.'

'Ay, a bunch of cripples most likely. Still, they can manage to dance. I hope our Stella doesn't get mixed up with one.'

'I don't suppose that would make any difference to her one way or another.'

'I might've knew you'd take her part. Allus do. I've only got to open my mouth and I'm wrong. But I'll say here and now, whether you like it or not, that I don't like her having too much to do with these men that crop up in her letters, whether they're a lot of pansies or Charles bleeding Atlas himself. It's not right. Before we know where we are she'll have one hanging round her neck wanting to get tied up – that's if she's lucky – and she'll be up the aisle and nobody stopping her. I know her. Nobody better. She'll not think we've got any say in it. But she'll have another think coming, I'm telling you. I'm not having her schooling till she's past twenty then ending up with bugger-all to show for it: married.'

'Most people get married some time, Hubert. You were keen enough.'

For a moment he was halted but those early days were too distant now, their vibrations levelling before they reached him. It was many years since he had paused by the school to approve of the wall he had repaired. 'And I'd been bringing a wage packet home to our mam damn near ten years afore that! I can't see Stella doing that. All the money it's cost us keeping her on at school and I'll be surprised if we see a penny of it.'

Alice did not speak.

'I expect you're saying it was your money that did it.'

'I didn't say anything.'

'You didn't have to; I know what was in your mind. You didn't need to earn it. We could of managed without. Our mam didn't go out. She stayed at home and looked after her family and took what Dad gave her and was thankful. Of course, she was a good manager; could make ends meet without looking for extras.'

She did not need to, at least not after I married him, tricking herself out in gifts from me which she had demanded, saying I could afford it, behaving as if it was her right.

'But whatever you're thinking, I'm still her dad. She does as I say. Have you seen this? "Last Sunday we walked by the river and further up there was a man fishing, looking very intense and serious. One of us tripped over his tackle as we were passing and upset his tin of maggots. He was very reasonable about it, but they were squirming through the grass and we had to collect them up. It was quite horrid. My hands did not feel right again until I got back and could give them a thorough scrub. Is Dad doing any fishing at the moment? I remember his claiming he had a special breed of maggots. I bet he would not have taken it so calmly if someone had scattered his with such an unwitting disregard for the paraphernalia of the mysteries of the fisherman's art." She's right there. She's a little devil, isn't she? She remembers. She used to like going fishing with her dad, nothing she enjoyed better, standing there as solemn as a judge with the rod I'd made her. I had to send her off for something and sneak a fish onto her line so's she wouldn't be disappointed. We had some good times.'

'Yes, you did.' Her pronoun was mechanical; the nerve no longer flicked.

'And will again when we have the chance.' Then as his eyes ran over the brisk farewells and rested upon the signature under which there were no symbols for kisses, his confidence cracked. He folded the pages and slid them

105

inside the envelope, smoothing down the torn flap as if lingering over a cherished memento. Round him the room spoke of her presence: a calendar she had made twelve years earlier and still hanging by the hearth; a tin money box with the paint scratched off round the slit; on the shelf an egg-cup shaped like a cockerel; an enlargement of a photograph of a girl laughing into the camera, saying his name.

'She was a fine little kid,' he declared bravely like a man bereaved.

'And she's grown up to be a young woman you can be proud of.' The conversation hardly engaged her; it was predictable as a stale habit.

'You can say that again,' he agreed. But the room was reticent about that, except for the letter with the faraway postmark. 'Someone to talk about.'

His wife did not answer and seeking a response to frighten off the silence, he regarded her for the first time that evening. Bent over her cup, she was tracing the jacquard pattern on the cloth with a finger, her hair like pale feathers drifting over her face. In that room with its irrevocable ghost, she was flesh, unchanging, a hope of warmth. He leant over her. 'But there's still us.' His voice curled with the old tenderness. 'She's mebbe gone, gallivanting to dances and up and down rivers, but that don't mean we have to sit moping. There's life in the old folks yet, isn't there? What do you say to us having a quick jaunt out?'

'I'm feeling too tired, Hubert.'

She had smiled. He could ignore the fact that her fingers did not answer the clasp of his. 'All right then, I tell you what, I'll go out and fetch you a bottle of Guinness – that'll put some strength into you – then I'll bank up the fire and we'll listen to the wireless, just the two of us, like old times, and then we'll have an early night. Best thing to do in the winter: keep warm and enjoy yourself at the same time. Kill two birds with one stone.' But the attempt to coax up a faded affection was hindered by a shudder as the ice of her hand stabbed his own.

'I'm sorry, Hubert, but I want an even earlier night than that. As soon as I've washed up the pots I'm going to bed.'

In the shed the air was distilled frost, his breath hanging in it like rime as he lit the storm lantern and made room for it on the bench. The frame of his bicycle, which he had intended to clean, radiated cold, blueing and numbing his hands which would not thaw in the weak warmth confined to the attenuated cone of light capping the lantern. Shrunk into his greatcoat, he stood by the bench and contemplated what the night had to offer. Back in the kitchen was a crackling hearth but the chairs before it were empty; in the pub were stools already occupied but the faces above them did not open for him. Round him the cold did not invigorate; it seeped through his clothes and lay on his skin like congealed sweat.

'I'll be stiff enough for them to lay me out soon,' he said to himself. 'Best go for a walk, to keep the old blood moving.'

Even alone in the shed he had to find an excuse.

'Why, look who's turned up. Hello, Stranger!' she greeted. Behind her a fire leaped and the old man slept in his chair. 'Thought they'd carted you off or something. Haven't seen you since before Christmas.' It was strange how, living so close, they knew so little of each other's movements.

'I've been a bit busy,' he mumbled.

'Ay, they allus say that. There's plenty to occupy a man in these parts, if he's not too fancy. Are you thinking of coming in, or were you just passing as usual?'

'I could do with a warm up.'

'There's the fire. I haven't got owt else.'

With flames warming his buttocks, he looked at the old man.

107

'He'll not bother you,' she interpreted. 'Used to like a bit of company but he don't know half what goes on now, do you, Grandad?' Through the thin tissue of sleep he sensed he was spoken of; the chalky lips spread tentatively. 'I'll be putting him to bed in a minute. It's nearly his time. Our Cliff's in bed, too. He brought a cold back from that school so I'm keeping him warm. Mind you, he kicked up a rumpus, being sent to bed.'

Hubert could not determine whether her words were simply chat or a promise of approaching privacy. 'Best place to be, this weather,' he experimented. 'I wouldn't say no myself.'

'Don't thee kid theesen,' she flashed, and the old man started; his head flung back and his eyes opened.

'What's that?' he cried out.

'Nothing for you to worrit over, Grandad.' She crossed to his chair. 'Time we had you in bed.'

'I'll not go yet. I like the fire. I no sooner get settled than you're after moving me. She makes a nice fire, the lass, doesn't she?' He spoke to where grey cataracts gave him Hubert's anonymous form. 'Only she's mean with the coal. Says it's short. I don't know what folks are coming to. It's not much to ask. I've a right to a bit of coal, my age. Wood's all right but it don't hold the heat, not like coal.'

'You be grateful for what you can get, and I don't ask you to do the chopping,' pushing an arm under one of his armpits and heaving. 'No, you keep away; he'll not let any'un but me touch him, obstinate old bugger. I'll bring you a cup of tea up, Grandad, when we've got you down,' she coaxed him towards the door. 'I shan't of course,' she said to Hubert as she stepped back for his cushion, 'else he'll be wetting the bed, but he allus thinks he's had it if I say.'

Hubert's hands were flexible again and his face rosy by the time the sounds in the bedroom above had ceased.

'He's getting a handful,' he said.

'Not one I can't manage.'

'Still, there must be things . . .'

'I have to hold it over the jerry, if that's what you mean, to make sure he hits it.'

'That's not a nice job.'

'Who else is there to do it? You tell me that. I haven't noticed folks offering. They don't come here visiting. Except when they want summat. And he's mine, for what that's worth. He wouldn't fetch much at the knackers. But he gave me a roof, didn't he? Not that he'd got any choice. So I'm not walking out on him now. You could say he's lucky. God knows what would've happened to him if I'd not dropped on him.'

'I reckon folks would've mucked in.' Hubert felt subtly implicated by her accusations. 'Neighbours.'

She snorted. 'Ay, poking their noses in to see what they could get out of it.'

'You're right there,' relieved of an embarrassing obligation. 'There's not a deal they do round here for nothing. But when our dad was took bad, back at home, the whole street got down to it. Worked it in shifts. "Have to do it that way; it's fairer," he said to me and he could hardly spit out for the coughing. "The lasses are that keen on the night work. Can't wait to get their hands on me." Allus try a joke, our dad would, even with his last breath.'

'Dirty bugger,' she approved.

With the fire heating his back and his feet planted firmly on the rug, Hubert looked at her. His eye, misting slightly at this recollection of street loyalty and friendship, gave him a woman who belonged to it, a woman of the kind he had known, not a slut as he had assumed though her hair was greasy and her nails were dirty and chipped, but a woman careless of appearances through defiant disregard of opinion, a woman who held herself now straight in his look, her face intense and her eyes shrewd.

'My God, it's blinking hot here. I'll have to take summat off,' and he began unbuttoning his coat.

'You're not forced to wedge yourself in front of the fire; nobody's asked you to stay.' Her integrity had already been nibbled at by their confidences; she was not ready for further threats.

'I'll bugger off right now if that's how you want it.'

'You can do as you like; nobody's stopping you. I wasn't thinking of staying up all night, myself, but if you're still interested in warming your backside you'd best make the fire up. I shouldn't have bothered.'

When she had spoken a log collapsed in the grate and he felt immediately a reduction in the warmth; as the old man had said, the ash did not retain the heat.

'I must say you're not very welcoming,' he declared, taking off his coat and bending to put another log on the fire.

'Welcoming! I don't know what I've got to feel welcoming about! Perhaps I should if I was in the habit of receiving company, but all I ever get thrown at me is a few words at the gate, in the dark.'

'People talk.'

'Who cares about that? I haven't seen you paying much attention to what folks have to say.'

'You can say that again,' he bragged.

'Damn the consequences and what's it matter what people think, is it? You don't even hold off having a girl when it suits you, do you? I've heard. You were lucky that little lot didn't get you into trouble.'

'It wasn't me. Couldn't of been. Must've been one of the lads at the factory.'

'But it could've been yours,' she persisted, 'so what's the difference? Like as not it would never have happened at all if you hadn't started her off.' Hubert blenched. 'Ay, that's made you think, hasn't it? I mean it. I know how it goes, none better. So why you suddenly start watching your p's and q's when it comes to having a few words with me, that's what I want to know.'

'There was nothing in it, I'm telling you. She was just a lass. I felt like a father to her.'

The woman laughed harshly. 'And I've heard that one before, too. Some men think we're crackers. But before they start flashing that idea around so much they ought to remember there's some families it goes on in.'

Hubert blushed at her coarseness. 'That's not something I know about. I say she was just a lass, to me. Do you think I'd get messed up with a girl who didn't know t'other from which?'

'Plenty do, and folks aren't so daft as not to believe it.'

'That's their business. Let them talk if they want, it don't hurt me.'

'If it don't hurt you, Lord Muck,' she jabbed quickly, 'why can't you have a few words with me without getting into a sweat? I'll tell you why not. Because it was all right having a village lass, ignorant as they come but keeping her legs together when she had the chance. That's not nice but still it's natural. Whereas, being seen with me, that's different. Word might get round that you went for dirt. And you wouldn't like that, would you? There's your high and mighty pride to consider. You wouldn't like people to think that you went beneath you.'

Again he blushed. Lamed, he answered, 'You aren't beneath me.'

'Nor ever like to be,' and laughed at her joke for, seeing him winded, she was happy. 'Well, now you've made

111

yoursen at home, I suppose you'll be wanting a cup of tea. I haven't anything stronger.'

'No, I don't want you to put yourself out for me,' he replied without irony. 'Come and sit yoursen down. Give yoursen a rest.'

She was surprised into compliance. 'I might as well. I don't have much time to enjoy my own fire. But I warn you I'm not staying long, so don't you be getting any ideas into your head.'

'I don't know what ideas I'd be getting. You tell me.' Looking down at her, he put his hands in his pockets and clenched his fists. The muscles hardened inside his sleeves. 'I'm not one for ideas, generally. I'm the sort that gets on with it.'

'You fancy yoursen all right. I don't know what for.'

'You casting aspersions?' He grinned. He had completely recovered ground now. 'It's not myself I fancy, but others do. And we won't mention what for.'

'You haven't half got a swelled head on you. Bloody Rudolph Valentino. They must be getting short, having to make do with you.' But as she accepted a cigarette and felt his leg lean upon hers, her own words mocked the creeping sensations which had so long lain dormant and which she could not now subdue; and seeing his eye probe under the slack edge of her overall whilst he bent over her with the match, she did nothing to hinder it, only remarked with a pretence at her former manner, 'You've only got one but it doesn't miss much, does it?'

'Not if it can help it.'

'They should've let you in the Forces, spite of it. They'ud have been doing some folks a service, keeping you out of mischief.' Her intention had been flirtatious but she saw his cheeks go slack and for a moment she was poised between what her mind recognized and her skin knew. She could have followed up her advantage, have pushed him away emasculated by his untested defeat, but the feel of him was upon her, his fingers spread over his thigh were already within her and a decision was made in which there was no choice. 'Still, it's mebbe as well they had to make do without you. There's plenty of other things you can turn your hand to, in a war.'

She was staring up at him, her chin jutting and teeth clenched, and he stared back, his blood pumping, his flesh struck with sweat. All the innuendoes and the conceit of veiled obscenities now confronted him and he could not determine whether the disturbance in his loins was that of lust or fear.

'What are you waiting for?' she demanded, and her face stiffened with bitterness that she should be reduced to a second invitation.

'You know what I'm waiting for.' His leer stretched on him ghastly like a mask. 'Reckon we've both knowed all along.'

Cornered, he fiddled with his cigarette, carefully flicking off the ash and stubbing the end against the bar of the grate. When behind him, the flame of the lamp which had been shrinking through their talk flamed up, wobbled and died in a gust of smoke. The glass globe was friezed with spears growing from ebony to points of sepia and ochre, and the wick bristled with fine sparks which fell away in a scurf of carbon.

'The wick's burning,' he said, moving quickly to the table to turn it down. 'Where's the paraffin? I'll fill it, but you'll have to wait till tomorrow when the wick's cold to trim it.'

'Leave it be.' She had risen; her fingers on his wrist stayed him. 'It's not that one I'm thinking of trimming.'

Bent on evasion, he was caught unawares and he laughed

outright, balancing on his heels, filling the room with the swirl of his pleasure.

Riding upon which, she was upon him, fingers prising out the stud at his throat, pulling at the tabs of braces, knotting over buttocks; other fingers over his dragged them under limp folds and into clammy crevices as she thrust out a thigh which found his member, rolled it until it was a solid fact between them, gasps leaving her mouth like snarls as her teeth gripped his neck. Sweat gushed from him, burst through his hairs and stuck to the sweat on her flesh now laid bare to him; one hand dug through the ooze of her wide hinterland; the other probed and scraped till her back jerked and she cried out in unsurfeited agony which he cruelly prolonged. For he was determined upon mastery, mastery of a woman whose passion had mastered the reluctance of his body and the prejudices of his mind and brought them to a single, piercing beam of heat, and, leaning all his weight upon her, he forced her towards the hearth and pushed her down in front of the fire.

There he crouched over her, his hands working fiercely while his eye, pricked by the firelight, saw it sheen the grease of her hair, shade off wrinkles, gild the carious teeth, spangle blemishes and lustre the moist down of a body which arched under him appealing for his mouth and twisting and ever widening in presentation for his thrust. Her hands were on him, kneading him as if she would milk him where he was, but confident, jubilant, he paused, enjoying a brief teasing interval before starting upon that which nothing would stop.

'You're nowt but a bleeding whore.' His voice caressed her.

'And I'll bet you've never had nobody do you so well.' Her words were a question, the cry of woman through the ages who, abandoned to the extremity of need, must believe herself unique, incomparable, without peer.

114

'You're telling me I haven't,' he assured her. It was true, and he answered out of the moment with no sense of betrayal. 'Here,' he said, 'you'll scorch,' humping her a little from the hearth. 'There'll soon be a smell of burning.'

'Who cares? You want to watch out yoursen.' Then she rose up at him and at last they were together, each fighting for his own, their bodies thumping, tossing, and he was exulting, calling her whore, dirty, parading herself under street lamps, raising her skirts behind cinemas, while she cursed him, swore at his size, shouted at him to go deeper, clawed at him, her nails raising weals on his back as she damned him for the alley dog he was.

'Now, give it now,' she urged. 'You're not fucking her bloody ink and chalk.'

Through his tumult her words reached him. Dazed and incredulous he saw beneath him the lips drawn back, the teeth bared, and in the glare of the fire to which their movements had brought them closer, her face was sharp, the skin taut parchment over the bone, while his, blistering in the heat, was suddenly pimpled with a rash of cold. His muscles went slack and his fullness curdled.

Not yet comprehending, she flexed to retain him and immediately his force slipped away and fell, slimed with the oil of her passion only, against her thigh.

'What's up?' she demanded, but as he sat back lifting his weight from her, she knew, and the explosion which had been denied her burst instead from her mouth.

'So that's it! You can't manage it! What's got into yer? After all your fine talk. My God, you've got some bloody cheek! You come here, swanking and making suggestions, preening yoursen like some bloody bull in rut, and I'm daft enough to fall for it. I should've knowed better.' Her hands were clutched between her legs; the chiaroscuro waves of the guttering flames swayed her kneeling form.

115

'I'm sorry. It just happened,' was all he could say, grappling with his clothes.

'Well, I've seen it all now. Some bloody fool I was, letting myself get messed up by a one-eyed bastard who can't even finish what he's started. Rolling about and screaming for it like some old maid who's never had it and can't wait to get it in.'

Defeated, he heard her contempt directed only towards himself, not towards the loss of her self-sufficiency, the pride of her bitter solitude.

So, 'It hasn't happened before,' he defended.

'No, I don't suppose it's had much of a chance. You acted as if you'd got plenty stored up.' Then as an explanation reached her, she scrambled up, crackling with outrage and fury, jabbing out words while her body gathered to spring. 'What bloody talk's that? You have the face to stand there and tell me it's my fault? I'm not good enough for you, is that it? Is that what turned the tap off? You're used to summat a bit high class, I suppose, doing her embroidery and humming hymns while you get on with it, Saturday night on the dot 'cos the sheet's turned Sunday, except when you need a bit extra and you have a simpleton behind a hedge who don't know enough to get into a lather and mucky up your shirt. That's what you're saying, but I can say too. Two can play at that game. You couldn't because you're frit. You haven't got the guts. It took you long enough to get here, scared fit to wet yoursen if she found out. You're nowt but a bloody sis tied to her apron strings. Like the rest of them. There's not a man I've knowed as can put up a fight and give as much as he takes and they expect you to pretend it's them is the boss! Some women don't mind but I can't be bothered. Not now. I want some'un with guts who knows how to fight and doesn't go soft at the

116

last minute. It's a good thing you've got that dicky eye. It suits you. You make me spit.'

He did not try to answer her. When she had finished he pushed his arms through his overcoat and without speaking left the house.

His own was dark as he approached but, still attentive to blackout and knowing that Alice was in bed, he expected nothing else, nor as he groped for the latch on the back door and found it open did he suspect anything unusual, until entering the kitchen he found the lamp on the table turned low and Alice sitting on one side of the grate. It was grey, banked with a fine drift of ash. Only a few cinders gleamed, fading, at the base.

'You've let the fire go out,' he greeted. It was his only dulled reaction to the still room.

'I know where you've been,' she said.

Hanging up his coat, he made no answer.

'You've been with that woman.'

'If you say so.' Exhausted, already beaten, he had neither the strength nor will for denial.

'Mr Hennell's been round. About something. He told me he saw you going in.'

'Then you'll have to take his word for it. Correspondent for the Managers. You'll believe him sooner than me.'

'You haven't said he's lying. I don't understand it. I don't know what to do.'

'I can't see as there's anything to be done.'

'Are you going to live with her?'

'God in hell, can't a man go with a woman without you thinking he's taking off?' Until that evening his answer would have swept him into a brawl; now it was little more than a spasm of irritation deadened by shame.

She nodded as if ticking off an item on a prepared list. 'Why did you do it, then? Why?'

'I don't want to talk about it.'

'But I do.' The reply was sharp. 'I've a right to know. I didn't ask questions about Enid. That was something *I* didn't want to talk about, but that woman is a different matter. Why, Hubert? How could you go with that woman – with her of all people?'

The question bewildered him. 'I don't know what you are talking about.'

'No, I don't suppose you do. You've never talked a lot with people in the village and you always shout me down when I try to tell you about my difficulties.'

'What's that got to do with it? I'm too tired for riddles.'

'Yes, you must be, but I expect it was worth it. You're always wishing for a good time. No doubt she gave you one.'

He winced at the irony and at the asperity and coarseness so unnatural to her. More than anything at that moment he wanted her gentleness; his misery desired the salve of her pliant understanding. He leaned towards her and stretched out his hands. 'Alice,' he begged.

She shrank away from him. 'No, no, don't touch me,' she rasped out. 'How can you? After . . .' and he saw on her face the fleeting energy of revulsion.

'It wasn't like that, Alice, really it wasn't. You've got it all wrong.' He was desperate now, desperate to hold her, to feel her hair clean and soft against his cheek, to stroke her white arms, to inhale her fragrance, to take the caress of her lips.

'I don't care a tinker's cuss what it was like, though I can bloody well guess. You bugger off after her if you want – if that's the sort you prefer now – only don't come crawling back to me afterwards, wanting it here. I've got some dignity left, though by God you've done all you could to destroy it, going off with a ruddy slut who has done everything in her power to humiliate me already. But I shall manage, bloody well have to, in spite of knowing that everyone else knows about it and is watching what I do. You can learn to bear bloody well anything in time.'

He looked at her appalled. 'Alice!' he exclaimed. 'Such language!'

She stared back at him but he could find no meaning in her face.

Chapter Eleven

'Mr Hennell's been round. About something. But he told me he saw you going into her house,' she had said.

Mr Hennell came round. About something.

About something.

Mr Hennell came round to explain about something.

She closed her eyes to shut out the picture of him standing nervously in front of her, and for a time she walked blindly down the private path left to the teacher, but he remained and she could not silence the words.

'I've come round about something a bit awkward.' He had blushed and refused a chair. 'It's our Jack. I don't want to do it, but I've got to think of him.'

The premonition of what he was about to say increased her heart's drumming but she held her back straight. 'He's doing very well, Mr Hennell. I'm hoping he will pass the scholarship. He is cleverer than his brothers, though of course they were never any trouble.'

They both looked away at her last word as from a sore publicly uncovered.

'Well, that's just it. I mean, there's not only the scholarship to consider though that's important and I'd like to think that one of them could do it, make something a bit extra of hisself, and let me say here and now, Mrs Gourley, if there's any teacher that could get Jack through, it's you and I mean that, sincerely I do. But somehow you think a bit more about the youngest, what's what, that is – not giving him more than is fair or liking him more, I don't mean that – but paying more attention, especially if he came a bit lateish like our Jack, not that I want you to think I've anything to say against the way you did with the other three. I don't want you to think that.'

He was lost in his search for palliatives; the point he had to touch was too painful for them both.

'They were all good boys, Mr Hennell.' The answer sounded to her like an epitaph on her career.

'Ay, and if they hadn't been, I'd have give them what for, not like some I can mention,' he replied with sudden spirit. 'And if you'll excuse me saying, Mrs Gourley, it would be better if you did now and again. It wouldn't do no harm and it might do more good than you'd care to calculate. Some of those big boys need a stronger hand and what they do is catching. I don't like having to say this but they would be better off with a man over them and that's why I've come to tell you I'm taking our Jack away.' At last it was said. 'I've had a word with Mr Drewy and he's willing to have him. The bike ride to Skellingford won't do him no harm.'

'I'm pleased that Mr Drewy has agreed, if that is what you prefer.' Her voice was tight; her hands were gripped together behind her back. 'I suppose he will have cleared the matter with the Office?'

'Oh yes, he said he would be seeing to all that.' His eyes slid away from her face like a guilty child's.

'Naturally I, also, will inform the Office of the alteration on the register.'

'I'm sure you will do what is in order, Mrs Gourley.'

'You were lucky that Mr Drewy had room.' For Jack. It was impossible to name him; to do so would have given flesh to her failure. She did not know how to ask the father to leave and he seemed stuck there, anxious to go but waiting to be dismissed.

'Yes, that's right, but it's maybe a bit easier for him, with the bigger school and having an assistant.' Relieved at the possibility of more neutral talk, the man relaxed. 'I've always said this one should have had another teacher years ago, but what with the war and so forth you can see why it got put off. It would've been no bad thing, especially if it had been a man.' He stopped abruptly and fiddled with the change in his pocket.

'It would have been a help,' she answered, trying to plump thin lips.

Encouraged by her agreement, he continued, 'And nice, whatever the teacher happened to be. It would have been some company. It would never have done for me, that school, even if I'd had the brains to be there.' The laugh was too boisterous and suddenly checked. 'I like a natter with my mates, between whiles. I was never happy over at Longholm crossing with only the bus driver passing now and again to exchange the time of day. You can have too much of your own company. It was a pity more of them evacuees didn't come and what did come didn't stop, else you might have got something out of that. Mr Drewy did. For a spell, that is.'

He stopped talking but she did not speak. 'Anyway, now with this new idea that's come in, the school will as like as not get smaller. They say they'll be carting all the big ones into secondary schools.' It seemed necessary for him to offer hope. 'They should've got rid of the older ones of yours before now, Mrs Gourley, like at Longholm, but it's a fair way for them to bike to Bingham and them pushed for room; and you allus managed so well. Manage,' he corrected himself. 'That's the way it allus is, show you can do summat and you're stuck with it.'

122

Again he paused but she could not respond. 'Well, as I say, when this new idea comes in they'll be forced to do something and I reckon there'll be a few you'll not be sorry to see go.'

'I think that is a long time ahead.' His presence was becoming unendurable. Never before had anyone presumed to comment on her work in this way. She took a step towards the door and waited.

'Well, I'd better be going,' he acknowledged her movement but did not stir. There was still something he had to say.

'I'd just like to mention, Mrs Gourley, that if there is ever anything I can do, any way I can be of help . . . I was wondering, well, I thought sometimes . . . you might be able to do with a bit of . . . Occasionally. Somebody official.'

His suggestion astonished and humiliated her.

He is insulting me. I don't know how he dare. First he takes his son away and now he is saying I could do with his help. A railway porter who hasn't set foot in a classroom since he was fourteen, thinking he can show me what to do, telling me how to run my school! I've been there over twenty years and nobody has ever interfered. Nobody has been interested. In any case, when you boil it down there is nothing anyone can do. It's up to you yourself in the end. There's nothing anyone could do. But he should not have said that to me. He has no right to speak like that. Making suggestions. It's disgusting.

'Mr Hennell, if you are insinuating that I am no longer capable of running my school, then I have to tell you that I take great exception to your remarks. You overstep your position. If you have any complaints to make, will you please make them through the proper channels.'

He stepped back, shocked and defensive. She was glaring at him as imperious and taut as a drawn bow.

123

'No, I didn't mean that. You've got it wrong. I wouldn't wish you to think that I was saying anything against you. I spoke in good faith.'

The strength of her profession cowed him. He was a boy again flinching before a cane poised to strike and, as she continued staring, frowning before the burst of chastisement, he tried to avoid it by a boy's means. 'I wouldn't have thought to mention it if it hadn't been for Mr Gourley. I saw him going into Amy Roe's as I came here, and knowing her lad can be a nuisance at times it gave me the idea he was mebbe putting in a word on your behalf, but I thought it might be best coming from one of the Managers.'

For a moment there was no alteration in her features or posture, then gradually her shoulders dropped, her eyes drew out of focus and her tongue crept over the tight lips. Neither spoke. A coal fell out of the grate into the hearth and lay blackening rapidly, emitting a scrawny thread of smoke.

'He was probably telling her she had a light showing,' he mumbled.

'No, and he wouldn't be seeing her about anything at the school, either. I never ask him to have anything to do with the school. In fact, we hardly ever discuss it. I think it is best to keep it quite separate.'

He had uncovered more than he could possibly have suspected. He had never seen a face so enervate, a rigid parody of life. 'Well, no doubt he had reason,' appalled at what he had done.

'I can't think of one.' His emotion came through to her and her eyes shifted slightly towards him. The proximity of shared suffering puzzled and alarmed her but she held to duty. 'Not a *good* one.' The mouth pulled back for the smile was a hollow in stone. He dared not look into it.

'You never know. Things aren't always what they seem.'

She did not answer.

'Look, Mrs Gourley, can I get you a cup of tea, make up the fire?'

'No, thank you, but that is kind.'

Then a hand had reached out and was taking hers which did not draw back. Together they looked down in bewilderment at their hands engaged in this strange ritual.

'I should never have mentioned what I did,' he said.

'I was bound to find out.'

For a time after he had gone she stood behind the closed door, holding the gift of his warmth against her cheek.

But that had died away now and there was nothing to replace it. Walking each day along the shunned path by the hedge of thorn, she was exposed to the slice of winds and the insidious creep of dank mist rawing her flesh. Inside the school, draughts from the grey playground were sharp as the grit pitting the floor under the iron tips of hard boots, and the fire seemed to recoil from her, sending its heat through flues and chimney, sucking at the cold then leaving it spread out round the meshed guard, a frosty aureole to its bright centre. But often even that was a still-born, smouldering thing left too soon by a caretaker growing negligent and she had to kneel in the flinty dust, take out the cold lumps, and with paper and sticks coax flames which gave her nothing; they were a formality she must honour. She put on more clothes; she hunched in front of the class buried in an overcoat, but her body would not thaw. It remained a narrow slab under the layers, traced for fissures. While in the cloakroom her hands leaped at the jab of ice sealing the water buckets and as she stood at the outer door her scalp tightened as shafts of winter rain entered with the children she had called.

'You mustn't cry.' She hugged a baby to her. 'I had a

little girl once and she used to cry when her hands were cold like ours. But she would sit on my knee like this and we would rub hands together like this and play pat-a-cake until they were warm again. Don't you want to play pat-a-cake? My little girl used to love playing pat-a-cake so much that I often had to pretend my hands were cold just so that she could play to warm them up for me. Perhaps when it snows it won't be so cold. Do you like the snow? I do very much. It is clean and pretty and hides all the dirtiness under a smooth, white sheet, and everything stays warm under the snow. Isn't that strange? Far away in another land the earth is always covered with snow. It stretches all over it like a carpet and the people who live there, who are called Eskimos, walk on top of it because they have big mats tied to their feet, called snow shoes. They wear thick warm fur suits and bonnets which leave just their faces showing and they build little round houses out of the snow and snuggle together inside and stay warm and cosy all winter long. Perhaps when the snow comes you will make a little round house like that, which is called an igloo, and you can be my little girl and we will go inside and keep ourselves cosy and warm. We shall be better off than little robin redbreast, shan't we? Can you say that poem after me?

"The north wind doth blow,
And we shall have snow,
And what will the robin do then, poor thing?
He'll sit in a barn,
And keep himself warm,
And hide his head under his wing, poor thing.'"

But she could not restrain the child longer. She slid off

126

her knee and ran away, looking back over her shoulder with wide eyes.

'You must take your plant with you,' she said to Jack. 'It will wither in the frost. But you must. It is yours. You grew it from a seed. It is something to do that. No, it does not matter if it does not bear a flower. It has already shown leaf. Indeed, it may do better than you expect. You remember the nursery rhyme?

"I had a little nut tree,
Nothing would it bear,
But a silver nutmeg
And a golden pear.
The King of Spain's daughter
Came to visit me,
And all for the sake
Of my little nut tree."

No, I cannot accept it from you; there is nowhere in my house that I could put it. You must take it to your new school, I'm sure Mr Drewy will find a place for it on his window sill. I hope you like it there, Jack. It will be good for you, a different school. It will give you a new outlook. You should always take the opportunity for that. One can become very set, staying in the same place.'

When the snow came the flakes were large and wet, spraying down like gob of the lingering mist and scumming the ground with sludge, phlegm-coloured over the spongy clay. Hail bruised her face; sleet whipped through a broken window in the classroom and lay stagnant, thick with ice and dust, upon the top of her desk. From the centre of the puddle she took up the stone which had been flung the previous evening and her fumbling discovered that the frost in her body had spread even to the tips of her fingers.

She saw this with relief. Numbed, she could no longer be hurt by scores.

But other senses were not thus protected. The cold in her brain was like metal upon which all sounds clashed stark, bare of texture, harsh notes which neither approached gradually nor softly diminished, striking the frigid disk in her head with cracking blows from mouths clanging: nine eights are seventy-two, nine nines are eighty-one, fourteen pounds one stone, hundred and twelve pounds one hundredweight, twenty hundredweight one ton, nine away from five won't go borrow ten nine from fifteen six nothing from four, four; softly along the road at ev'n in a twilight lit with gold wrinkled with age and drenched with dew old Nod the shepherd goes; i comes before e except after c, words ending with y knock off y and add ies; thirty days hath September, April, June and November; down came the raindrops and washed poor Incy out; please Mrs Gourley the clock's stopped, Mrs Gourley the bus has gone past, please Mrs Gourley Des kicked me going home to dinner; a Glaswegian comes from Glasgow, Taffy was a Welshman, Taffy was a thief, Taffy came to our town and stole; please Mrs Gourley Ivy's sock's scorching on the fender; red orange yellow green blue indigo and violet; please Mrs Gourley Ken Marriott's knocked my paint water over, please, Mrs Gourley, John Holt wants to go;

> "Now the day is over,
> Night is drawing nigh,
> Shadows of the evening,
> Steal across the sky,
> Jesus give the weary,
> Calm and sweet repose,
> With thy tender blessing,
> May mine eyelids close."'

Until the noise trapped in her head swelled and battered against the bone. She crushed it between her hands, shouting to the class to stop, but the clamour would not cease. Even when she sent the older boys outside sometimes in the middle of a lesson in the hope that the room would become quieter, their remembered voices still crashed against the echoing glacier in her brain; yet their stridency was only a part of the dissonance she could not release, and sense was spun upon revolutions of brutal sound.

Whose insistent vibrations were counterpointed by another rhythm, the rhythm of sporadic sobs which would burst from the frightening thickets on the perimeter of the resounding centre, then be jerked back, controlled to shallow quavering but impossible to repress. They rose upon words unspoken, imagined, distorted, peopled with shapes malformed and dirty, decked out with colours bizarre and lurid, of a woman scarlet and glowering, of orange teeth biting, of fire dancing macabre behind soiled stockings opening, of braces dangling at knees grinding on a blood-red floor where dust slid away from the bellows of mottled bodies which never separated but remained fastened together, sometimes rolling into the indigo shadows where she could not see them but known by their rocking movements and grunts which began to drown the other beats and sounds in her head as, turning once more at her feet, the bodies yellowed and fuzzed by the smoke of tobacco went on and on disregarding her presence, lips frothing, backs straining, clawed hands tearing through taboos and mouths leering. At her, as she stood in a classroom swayed by the wind flapping her charts and pictures and pushing against charred rafters; at her, surrounded by eyes which peered under lifted curtains, which watched through chinks in doors, which waited above desks, their holed centres distending and contracting to the rhythm of that greased mating which continued on and on until the faces at the desks slanted with knowledge, faces with lips bold and grinning, with fangs bared like vampires', with mouths stained with caries, issuing crudities and insidious corruption which spurted out at her feet in a scalding nauseous slime from which vapour rose to fill her nostrils with an acrid stench. And as the two sucked together then fell apart, she saw through the mist which leaked crack by crack into the roofless room, a single eye, glazed, unmoving, sinister, set to regard her with unalterable expression, as incapable of perception as it was ignorant of what had been done.

But the other eyes knew, and her own could not meet them. To the jangling against the iced metal, the pumping in the shadow, was now added the scratch of sniggers, and her body, numb under its many layers of cloth, was exposed to their contemplation, laid out for assessment of its deficiencies which had lost her the man. Disobedience lifted her skirt and mocked her cold thighs. Insolence squeezed her waist and patted her slack belly. Rudeness tweaked at her blouse and fingered her thinning breasts. Ungovernable rowdiness scoffed at the grey in her hair.

She crept through the class, admonishing where she could, teaching where she was permitted, or sat behind her high desk staring at the derelict room while the children shouted and fought for long hours round the crumbling walls. When, called in by a monitor, they again crowded upon her, she retreated, steadying herself against the blackboard, and she selected passages at random out of text books for them to copy out, let the babies play with crayons or string beads, and set the older ones to work through endless exercises which she never checked for she could not touch the books. She shrank from them as she shrank from the pressing bodies, the smell, the grimy

130

hands, the looks in the prying eyes. She shrank back among the tumultuous visions twirling on the pivot of iron sound. To these she was subject; she was a medium responsive to their whim; she moved to their drumming; speaking, she spoke with their voice. Loathsome, monstrous, they inhabited her and became her own; bereft of all else, she abandoned herself to their feral power, yielded beside their obscene union, and like a mother nursing a deformed thing she can neither love nor forsake, in hatred she kept her repulsive spirits close, but jealously, resisting intruders.

And when one more insistent than the rest clutched at her sleeve, whimpering, 'I kept asking, Mrs Gourley, but you didn't tek no notice,' she thrust him back and, as he knocked against the desk, saw the faeces of curdled brown ooze down a thigh. 'They was getting on to me,' the sallow face whinnied. 'They pinched my pebbles. Cliff Sidebottom chucked them in the ditch.'

Her images, startled, began to recede. She closed her eyes, frantic to recall them. They were hers, of her, the sole pulse of her mind, but they were being pushed away by a repellent face which seemed to be claiming from her some sort of duty, by a body friable as fungus, flaccid beside their flexed energy, a body suppurating pus. The sounds in her brain coalesced and leaped to one high, screeching note.

'Why do you come to me?' She was bearing down upon it. The body was cringing against the fire guard. 'Why don't you go out?'

'I daresn't. I asked. They wouldn't let me go.' Stretched out against the mesh, the whole body leaked.

'I've told you not to wait. I've told you to go out as soon as you feel it coming. Why can't you hold it, you stupid, stinking, filthy beast?'

The ruler in her hand came down flat on a shoulder. It jumped, taking the body with it. Saliva looped from a

131

mouth whining, 'Please, Mrs Gourley, I didn't do it a purpose,' and more brown squeezed out and splattered at her feet.

Then the ruler was smacking the blunt head; it poked at the soft belly, struck the skinny arms, and a tongue hung loose from a mouth gurgling gob as the body jerked and slid, trailing thick droppings upon which she skidded while the ruler twisted in her palm and the edge sliced at the striped legs, hit the squelching trousers and drew across uplifted wrists. He was a slug contracted to a hump at the toe of her shoe, turning to brown foam under the jet of her salt, and as she cut at him, finding patches of bare flesh he could not protect, she discovered under her blade two other bodies which now returning she could at last beat and batter into the dirt they occupied, could triumph over their weals and cries for mercy, could gloat over them submissive to her power. Until, pausing, she was aware of silence.

The shriek had gone from her head. She was in a room lit palely by a winter sun. In front of her children were sitting. They were still and uttered no sound. The only sound came from a boy on the floor. He was weeping and his hands were over his thighs, trying to conceal a shameful mess.

'Get up, Holt,' she said, 'and clean yourself up. I will get a clean pair of trousers out of the box.'

She opened the door for him and he scrambled out, and as she turned to the rest she saw the shock on their faces.

'We will do some reading round the class for a change,' she told them.

Quickly they got out their books; one ran to the cupboard and fetched her copy. No one objected to her choice. There was no chattering while those selected stood up and read. They sat quietly when John knocked and she handed him the clean pair of trousers. No one scoffed at him when he returned to his seat. When she sat at the piano to play the final hymn she knew that behind her everyone was standing perfectly ordered and that nobody giggled or nudged.

Her images had been expelled; the ice in her brain was quiet. But what had left her had not been replaced by caressing warmth. It had been replaced by fear in her children's eyes.

'Are you badly or summat, love?' Hubert asked.

She was sitting crouched in a chair, far away from the fire left unkindled, and there was no meal ready.

'I'm all right.'

'You give me a shock in the dark like that. I didn't know what was up. You're not telling me there's nowt the matter.'

'There's nothing.'

'Have you got a touch of the 'flu or summat? That school's like a colander for draughts.'

'I might have a cold coming,' she obliged.

'Well, it's no good hanging about waiting for it. I'll have a go at this fire then we'll get something warm inside you. Can't have you cracking up – don't know where we'd be.'

'I'd better see to the tea. No, please don't worry, I'm not an invalid.' Allowing him to help her with her coat, she did not flinch.

'I must say you're looking very down.'

'Perhaps you should not have lit the lamp.'

'I'll nip round to the pub after and fetch some rum. A bowl of bread and milk with a measure of rum in it'll soon settle that cold, if that's what it is. It seems more'n a cold to me.'

'I don't suppose it is.'

'You look more miserable than out of sorts. Has owt gone wrong?'

'No, it's been the usual kind of day.'

133

'It don't look like it. Have them kids been playing up? Reg Hennell stopped me on the way to work a bit back and he said he thought you was having a spot of bother, some of the big lads causing trouble and it might be getting on top of you. Said it was a pity you'd no one to call to. You can imagine what I said to that. Gave him a real mouthful. Told him it was none of my business, nor his neither, interfering bugger. I sent him packing. "She's needing advice from nobody and especially not you," I told him. "She's got more nouse in her little finger than you've got in your whole head, or anybody has round here, and there's nothing these lads could get up to she doesn't know how to deal with; there's nowt they can do as hasn't got whiskers on it as far as she's concerned. She knows all the tricks," I said.'

'That's right.'

'All the same, I suppose they can still take it out of you. You don't look yourself, Alice, and that's a fact. I don't like to see you looking like this. It's upsetting.'

'I'm sorry.'

'I mean it. You shouldn't come home so washed out. It's not right. You didn't used to. Blinking hell, I remember when Stella was a babby you'd be bouncing about seeing to her and getting tea and pickling and jamming like wild fire, and up again before it was light cooking breakfast and fetching in water, singing and banging.'

'That was a long time ago.'

'And you had time for a bit of fun; you'd never say no to going on the razzle, pictures if we wanted or over to Skeggy for a paddle in the summer. Used to have some high old times.'

'That was before the war.'

'I know that; not much chance of going on the spree now, but it's got so's you wouldn't if you could, and now things out there are looking up it doesn't seem as if you've got it in you.'

'We all have to grow older.'

'It's not that. Damn it, I don't feel no different to what I did when I was courting. It's that bloody school. You come home like a wet rag. It's not like me to say, I know, but if there's any of those young 'uns you want sorting out, you just tip me the wink. I'll give them a few stingers they'll not forget quick, no kidding.'

'That won't be necessary. I already have.'

'Well, I'll be damned! How long've you been keeping that up your sleeve? I thought it was summat you never went in for.'

'It was, but I have.'

'And did it put paid to them?'

'Yes.'

'What have I allus told you? They could've done with it a long time ago. You were allus too soft. Kids are like everyone else, they need to know who's boss. So you can let fly now and again, like your old man, can you? And I never knewed! Kept it to yoursen all these years! Like an old Jew. My God, Alice, fancy turning up summat like that after twenty years! Here, come and give us a kiss.'

She obeyed. There seemed no reason now why she should not.

'Your hair's still nice. I suppose you're talking about these grey 'uns when you say about getting old. They don't matter. Are you taking after me in your old age, then, lashing out? I'll have to be careful.'

'Probably.'

'I can hardly credit it. I'd like to see you. Wish I'd seen them kids jumping. I bet you made a good job of it. That's one thing about you, do everything proper once you start, never anything by halves. But it's taken it out of you, hasn't it? Mustn't let that happen, even if you've got me to cuddle you when I get home. Don't you worry yourself. You'll get used to it after a bit.'

'Yes,' she answered.

Chapter Twelve

My dearest darling little Stella,

     Thanking you for letter received last Thursday week
and pleased to have your news and hope your behaving
yourself and not up to anything your old dad wouldnt do,
thats a laugh just watch him if he had the chance. Is
there a letter from that girl of mine I say when I get in
and I must say when it comes its worth waiting for I prop
it up against the sugar while I have tea and then I take it
out to the lav and sit there by myself having a good read,
better than the paper any day. Last one, second time
round, I had to finish off holding the torch to it and I
thought enybody see me now with my trousers round my
ankles with a torch would say Id gone off my rocker. Still
theres one born every day. It will be a shock getting one
from your old dad wont it, just wait till she opens this I
said to myself, shel'l think the worlds coming to an end
getting a letter from her dad, he has never been one
much for writing and hasnt much idea how to go about it
except put the words just as they come, not like his
daughter who can tie them together like a book and even
knows how to get you laughing when she wants to. We
didnt see much of you in the summer holidays gadding
about so much but its nice to have friends and enjoy
yourself while your young I always say, you didnt get

much chance to get to know whats been going on and
Alice always perks up when she sees you and would not
say anything for the sake of not worrying you even if she
wanted, you know your mother, can shut up like a clam
and wild horses wouldnt drag her if shes stuck her heels
in, I dont know if you thought she looked alright but she
still keeps herself tidy and powders her nose when you
come and I dont want to be the one to cause you any
upset but she hasnt been herself recently and now its got
so she cannot keep on. I reckoned it up that when the
warm days were with us again and with the War ending
like it has she would come out of it, the last six years
what with rationing and such like are bound to have got
her down and theres been a spot of trouble at school, but
I dont know what that was about in so many words, you
know me not one to stick my nose in where its not
wanted and it seems she sorted them little buggers out
excusing my language, but you know your old dad
straight out and no messing, months back that was and I
thought that was the end of it but she never seemed to
pick up. To tell you the honest truth Stella she got worse
and Ive tried all I can to make her snap out of it but half
the time shes not even listening and the other half she
doesnt take notice. Ive been near the end of my tether
some weeks which is saying something for your dad, not
being the sort that goes in for worry, leave that to others
I always say that have got time for it. To cut a long story
short and not waste paper as the jew boy pleaded with
the chemist, it got so I could hardly do anything with
her, come home at night and find her sitting on the floor
staring at nothing and wouldnt say why, and not eating
enough to keep a sparrer going and just picking at things
I tried on her, eggs whipped in milk and Guinness topped
up with milk to put her on her feet, my grandma swore by

138

it, and I told her once it seemed she was set on starving herself to death and do you know what she said, she said she wouldnt mind if she did. That fair scared me out of my wits and Ive still got a few though I know you'll not believe it, it did, Im not kidding, and I reckoned it was time she saw a doctor, give her a tonic or something to liven her up. Is she worried about anything he said, shes in full time work isnt she, it wasnt old Doctor Phillips but a new one just started to help him out, Doctor Phillips would not have bothered asking questions, taken her pulse and known without any fuss, been at it for years, saw you into the world and made a good job of that, though he wouldnt have had a chance would he if it hadnt been for your old dad. How is she managing at work, he asked, she has the full responsibility of the school doesnt she, and I near as nothing showed him the door at that, but I bit it back and told him there was nothing to worry about there, and as it happened I knew what I was talking about because a few weeks back I took the afternoon off and dropped into the school unexpected, I'll say it was unexpected since I hadnt set foot in the place since I was courting, just to check on what might be going on, and it was like the grave, kids working like niggers and you couldve heard a pin drop, getting up like a troop of soldiers when I opened the door and saying good afternoon like they had one voice between them. My God, but you've got them well drilled I said to Alice but all she could do was nod and ask why Id come. I told that to the new doctor and I must say that put him back a bit but he didnt go and he didnt say he would be sending young Robinson out with a tonic either, but he kept asking questions I didnt think had anything to do with him, he is a young chap, just out the Army and full of new fangled notions, talking fancy with

139

words youd have a job getting your tongue round and spitting out, and the upshot of it was he said she had to go into hospital. I said, well, if they can get her eating again and give her a proper rest, then I had no objection, and then it turned out it wasnt the General he was talking about but Bingford Park. Thats where they cart off the loonies I said, I was beside myself, I really was. Dont imagine, he says with the sort of smile that makes you want to put a bunch of fives in his kisser, dont imagine they are all in strait jackets and padded cells, then looking at me straight and in a nasty way he said, you wife has no need of those, she has got her own already. Well Im not kidding I near knocked him for six, what you trying to suggest by that, I said, and he said summat about it being obvious and went into a long rigmarole about shock and stress and suppressing whatever it was and I didnt understand half the time what he was getting at and I said all she needed was a good tonic and Doctor Phillips would have thought twice afore saying it was Bingford Park she needed at which he gave me a look like he was ordering the firing squad and said he was not suggesting it without thought but I was entitled to a second opinion and he would send someone else in. Then suddenly Alice sat up and said sshe would go and you could have knocked me down with a feather, after all I'd done to keep her out, and he said she was very wise and he had a friend who had just started there who knew all the latest ideas so it looks to me as if the bloody Army's taking over, no sooner out of barracks theirselves than they're hell bent on getting other folks in. I took her there a week last Sunday and I visited Saturday and honest to God Stella it was more than I could stand seeing her there in bed with a row of folks eyes staring like fish and one old girl with sides like a cot to the bed rattling and whining and Alice saying it didnt matter to her being there, and me not being able to tell my mates at work. I cried all night when I got home, I couldnt help it. I did all I could to keep her out Stella. If it hadnt been for Alice saying that Id never have let her go but that young doctor took what she said as final I couldnt stop it. So dont blame your old dad, will you. They wouldnt take notice on me, and I had to send you a letter though I put off writing. I know youll feel ashamed like I do but its a cross well have to bear. Ill be taking her a clean nightie every week and seeing that she doesnt want for anything I can provide for her, my poor Alice, the best wife a man ever had and always so clever, make a good job of anything she turned her hand to, and lying there in a row of loonies. I cant write any more without crying. I expect a letter from you when you can manage one.

Your ever loving and broken hearted dad.

'I want to visit her.' There were rings on the table from the previous glasses. Behind them someone had begun to hum the melody of 'Foggy, foggy dew'.

'Of course. I'll go with you.'

'Do you really mean that? It's a long way.'

'Exactly. It would be an even more unpleasant journey if you went by yourself. I'll borrow the old man's car; he has a special petrol allowance.'

'You don't have to feel obliged.'

'I don't feel the least bit obliged.'

'I can't understand it.'

'What was she like last vac.?'

'I suppose she was quiet, but then, I did most of the talking, and I can't have been at home long, when I work it

141

out. It seemed long enough. There's absolutely nothing to do there, you know. You honestly can't imagine.'

'Don't you be so sure. I spent six weeks in a billet in the Shetlands. After the scenery all there was to fall back on was NAAFI beer.'

'That was something.'

'Admittedly some compensation, but I can think of better ways of spending my time.' From men she had known the previous session the innuendo would have been a hopeful brag; from him it was a casual truth tempered by cynicism and impatience at other things his Service years had imposed. 'What were you doing when you weren't at home?'

'I spent five or six weeks at the Burtons, then we all sort of camped out on Diana's uncle whose house is far too big for him anyway.'

'I get the picture.'

'It wasn't like that. You are an odd man – all this experience of things I can only read about and then suddenly, crack, a sort of petulant jealousy.'

He laughed. 'Whatever should I be jealous about? I don't think jealousy is one of my passions and I certainly have not met anyone to inspire it.' Seeing her cheeks flush, he added, 'You choose the wrong word. It's envy. I believe I could have enjoyed your summer vac. but I was born three years too soon, and those years left me with rather a different way of seeing things.'

You gave them your concern, sympathy, affection, even horror, swabbing the blood, listening to the ravings, but you did not let it permeate to your centre; that must be protected, kept whole and unaffected; and when you gave women your attention it was not a ripping passion justified by months of celibacy and the clock on the wall, but an attention as clinical as mopping up vomit, as inserting the syringe.

142

'Tell me what you remember about your mother this summer.'

'She didn't appear odd in any particular way. She wanted to know about everything I was doing. Very interested in the course and said she would like to read some of the books if I would leave her a list but I forgot. I suppose there is no point now. We went for walks a lot, at her suggestion; it was gorgeous weather and generally we were out all day, just taking a bag of apples from the garden. When we got tired we would lie in the sun and I read and she napped. It was nice. She didn't seem to bother about cleaning. That reminds me. One evening when I went into the house after reading in the garden I came upon Dad dusting the living room. "Just putting a duster over the furniture," he said. "Have to keep it bright and cheerful while you're here." He hardly ever did anything in the house, but I don't know whether it was significant. It is hard not to interpret things now in the light of his letter.'

'Why shouldn't you?'

'There are plenty of things he has reason to be silent about.'

She had not shown him the letter from her father. Had she offered it to him he would have refused, both through respect for its intimacy and the wish to avoid that kind for himself which, from his acceptance, might be assumed.

'Did she mention her school?'

'I can't remember her doing so. Nor did I see her doing any work for it. She usually spent a lot of time in the summer holiday preparing stuff, all manner of things – charts, craft work for the boys and sewing for the girls, cutting out pinnies and nightgowns, that sort of thing. I imagined she had done it before I came home.'

'She obviously tried to see as much of you as she could

while you were there. It sounds as if you had a pleasant time together, lounging about in the sun.'

'Yes. She enjoyed that. Once she said she liked being right away, outside under the trees where there were no eyes on you.'

'What did you say to that?' he asked quickly.

'I made some joking comment that, to hear her talk, anybody would imagine she contemplated some interesting indiscretion. We're on those sort of terms; it's ages since I have thought of her as as mother to whom you have to be careful what you say.'

'And she?'

'Drew in her lips and looked prim so that I thought I had overstepped the mark for once, then she said that there were worse things than indiscretion, but you had to learn to live with them if you could. Still, she said she felt easier lying on the grass with the air brushing her face; you couldn't blame anyone for doing that. Whatever else happened, the grass always bounced back when you got up and the air and the sun stayed the same. Then she said she wished it were warmer and honestly I was boiling.'

'It sounds as if she were trying to tell you something. Did she say anything else like that?'

'I agreed that we should enjoy the sun when we could but that I didn't see why anyone should be blamed for it and she said she hoped I never would and that was that. Nothing on earth will make my mother talk if she's determined not to.'

He looked across at her. The face was intelligent, not pretty but with small bones, the skin like a child's, unetched by signs which the years lay down for the curious seeker. Dispassionately he considered the mouth and wondered at the resolute privacy of the sick woman now repeated in the unwrinkling line of her daughter's lips. Perhaps, he thought, she dare not risk contagion from another's pain.

'And you never tried any more?' he asked, knowing he was accusing himself.

'How could I? She obviously didn't intend to say anything else and it wasn't for me to press her. Why should I suspect it was all so important, which is what you're suggesting, isn't it?'

He watched the toss of the head, the dismissive shrug, the arrogant self-absorption of youth.

'That's what it looks like. From the outside.' Without seeing, he reached for his glass and found as he tilted it to his mouth that it contained only a lining of froth.

'I don't know how I could be expected to realize that.' She had tried to describe it, had tried to reconstruct those days, had remained calm and quiet while her mother lay in Bingford Park, defeated by the disgrace of a husband's conduct which she was too loyal to discuss with her daughter; and now this man from whom she had expected interest and sympathy was asking questions, saying it was all her fault. 'I think I shall have to go. I don't want to talk about it any more or deal with your interrogation.'

He leaned forward and caught her wrist. 'I'm sorry. It is a kind of professional habit; I suppose you could call it that,' and averted his head because of the lying excuse.

Then regarding her again, he saw her face was no longer unmarked; it mapped out a terrain whose symbols upon others he had chosen to ignore. But he did not turn away. 'Can I ask one more question? Please. Then we'll go. Better to cry outside if we can manage it.' Behind, they were singing, 'So I took her into bed, And I covered up her head, Just to save her from the foggy, foggy dew.' On top of the damp table his hand was over hers. He could feel the bones ridged under his palm. 'When you loved her so much, why did you stay away?' It was suddenly essential for him to know.

'Because I did not get on with my father. Because he treated her badly and a few years ago I came to the conclusion that my presence made it worse.'

What he saw as she hesitated at the door of the ward was a man with greying sideburns, who held a paper carrier like a bag of tools, stoop over a woman propped against pillows and smooth the hair back from her forehead; and he saw the woman lift a hand from the coverlet, take the other's and hold it to her cheek, and he watched the man bend to kiss the eyes she had closed as she grasped him, and he saw the new-pressed crease in the trousers of the Sunday suit flatten and the stiff white collar fastened to the striped flannelette of the working shirt poke forward as, without disturbing his position, the man felt with his free hand for the chair by the bed and sat beside her; then the younger man saw the other slide an arm under the woman's neck and saw her head rub backwards and forwards against the cloth before slipping to nestle into the shoulder. Until the daughter at last felt she could leave the door, and the man whom they had accompanied raised his face to them across the bed.

After her puzzlement at the visit of her daughter, her diffident pleasure, the introduction, and the explanation of his presence, talk wavered. There was no surgery to describe, no stitches to show off, no hopeful calculation concerning homecoming, none of the tough buffoonery peculiar to hospitals to relate, no ward characters to appreciate among the desolate beds.

'Everyone is very kind,' she said, 'and Sister says I'm not here to be punished but to be made well again. That was good of her, wasn't it? I felt like crying when she said that. The doctor points out that a lot of people don't get what they deserve anyway, but I don't think that matters.' She blinked as the sun found her face and frowned at them

146

through its sharp light. 'It is nice of you all to come and see me. It is considerate of you to bring Stella,' she addressed him, 'but I am sorry to have given you the trouble.'

Next to them two nurses clucking rebukes raised a parchment body and drew away soiled sheets.

'I've brought you a clean nightie,' Hubert said, and pulled it out of the carrier bag. 'I freshened it up with the iron but I had the devil's own job with the lace.'

'Isn't it pretty?' she asked them. 'I made it just after we were married. It has been a good nightie, hasn't it?'

Outside he waited while the other man retched without the relief of vomit. 'I can't stand seeing her there. My Alice! I would never have believed it could happen. She seems to have given in.'

'She will be receiving the right help.'

'Help for what? I don't know what's wrong with her. You don't understand. It's terrible, seeing your wife in a place like that.'

'They will cure her.'

'I hope to God you're right. Her and Stella are all I've got.' Then, as they still waited for his daughter. 'You're her new boy friend, then, are you?'

'We're both around.'

'Just missed the war, then.'

'No. I was called up in forty-two.'

'You're not saying! I would never have thought it!' Over the bonnet of the car the man was reassessing him, his expression wary. 'They wouldn't have me, blast their eyes, because of this,' tapping his pot shell, 'though believe me I can see as much with the other one as you can with two any day. I lost it fishing a cartridge out of the fire that our Stella, silly little nipper, had just thrown in. Got between it and her just in time, else she would've got it, 'stead of me.' Across the bridge of his nose the moving eye slanted

147

slyly. 'She'll never forget that. Whatever she says about her old dad, she knows that if it hadn't been for him, she would have been messed up like he was. Nobody else can ever do the same for her, and she knows that, though she never says. It makes a difference, you'll see that. She'd never let anyone come between her and her old dad.'

The two men confronted each other over the glinting metal. The younger kept his face blank of the dislike he was feeling, while his brain sang with a decision made.

'What did you say you were in?' Hubert could be more relaxed now.

'Army Medical Corps.'

The other grinned, happy. 'So you wouldn't see any of the action.'

'I was there for some.' Michael paused, then deliberately, holding the man's sight, he added, 'Still, I suppose you could say I didn't see much of the action. Merely the results.'

Chapter Thirteen

'A man's been, saying they'd be bringing him round at half-past one,' Mrs Livesey greeted them as they stepped into her hall. 'He asked was it only the one car. I said yes if that was what you'd ordered.'

'That's right, Mrs Livesey,' Michael answered.

'I'll have to leave you at twenty past to catch the bus so when they've fetched the flowers down I'd be glad if you'd spang the door after you.'

'You mustn't do that. We are expecting you to travel in the car with us.'

'I must say that is very nice of you but I don't know that I like to. It's not right, somehow. It's for family.'

'Not at all. There will be plenty of room. In any case, you have been family for the last ten years.'

'I suppose you could say that.' Her eyes, already inflamed, were again glazed with tears. 'Come into the warm then, while you wait. I've put the flowers in his old room. I couldn't have them down here with him gone.'

'If you don't mind, I should like to see them,' his daughter spoke for the first time.

'You do as you think fit, my dear,' the older woman answered and remained standing by the door of her kitchen while the others went upstairs.

The room was cleared now and anonymous. Its air smelt

stagnant, waiting to be stirred. On the table the colour of the flowers was incongruously festive, deceiving the eye to forget that the blooms, hot-house forced for the grave, had been cut and brutally wired and would soon wither fittingly. One wreath was formed like a cross, the other was a large orthodox ring. On the card attached to the first was written: In memory of Mr Gourley a dear friend from Mrs Livesey. The card on the second was blank.

'You must write something on it,' he said.

'What does it matter?'

'But you can't leave it like this. The whole business is unavoidable. This is part of the ritual.'

'There is no one to read it.'

'Mrs Livesey will,' he answered without humour, and held his diary under the card while she wrote: From Michael and Stella. 'And the children?'

'That's enough,' she said, then touching a stiff toupee of petals as synthetic as if they had been moulded in resin, 'I can't bear these. Can you remember Mother's? I think just about everyone in the village must have brought some; there were too many to go on the bier and the church was packed.'

'They respected the service she had given them.'

'And he, he was practically hysterical. We had to support him, when all the time I couldn't forget what he'd done.'

'I know. But I've often wondered whether there was more to it than that. The first time we visited her he was very upset and I took him out to that old car of Dad's I'd borrowed. You stayed with her. She told you something then, didn't she?'

'She made some complimentary remarks on you.'

'So you've said. But that wasn't all.'

'She talked a bit, but I was very muddled about what she meant. It was very intimate.'

150

'They're both dead, Stella.'

She was silent, plucking at the flowers under her hand.

'Stella, listen to me. They're dead. Tell me and let them go. Please.' He was pleading for them all.

She did not answer.

'I think I'll have a word with Mrs Livesey,' he said at last. 'Perhaps I should have ordered a second car. She and I could have travelled in it together.'

As he reached the door, her voice stayed him. 'She said things about you. She took to you; she liked you though she could never know you.' He turned and waited. 'I can't explain what she said. I have never been able to work it out.'

Her back was to him and she spoke into the empty hearth. 'She remarked on your eyes. They were a nice colour and they didn't look at her in that way. It was the eyes, she said, that she had not been able to stand. Afterwards. I didn't know what she was referring to but I didn't interrupt. It was intolerable, the difficulty she had telling me. She said it was the same as her brothers had looked when he was thrashing them. He wouldn't touch her because she was a girl, but he would take his strap and beat them and they kept their mouths tight shut and never cried out, but she saw their eyes. She had vowed never to do it but he made her, pulling at her like that when there was the noise and they were both there on the floor, dirty and disgusting, and after she had done it they both went, and the noise; but that did not finish it because it was there in their eyes, just as it had been when he had the strap out. So, she said, she was as bad as him really, and he had admired her for doing it.'

She finished. Neither spoke. For twelve years she had kept this from him and he knew the effort it had cost her.

'She would have forgiven you for telling me, Stella. It seems that she liked the look of me.'

She turned. 'It was terrible for her, wrenching it out. So private.'

'I know that, though I don't know what she meant. But I'm pleased you've told me. Thank you, Stella.'

Its meaning and the pain it would bring him were irrelevant. At that moment he felt gladness that she had given up to him the last flick of her ghosts, and as they regarded each other across the room, its chill was stirred and warmed by the wreaths' russet glow.

Someone knocked on the door. 'I've come for the flowers, Ma'am,' he whispered then, seeing them on the table, leaned out and shouted over the bannister, 'You needn't bother coming up, Dennis; there's only two,' before reassuming his cadaverous mask and mincing across the room with his black greatcoat flapping at his calves. The wreaths held against him like bright prey soon to be pecked at, he intoned furtively, 'We're ready when you are, Sir,' and left, a professional spectre.

Downstairs Mrs Livesey was waiting. 'It's no good. I can't come. Him coming back like this, laid out in a coffin. He was no ordinary lodger to me and I can't go and see him being taken off to be burnt up. He allus wanted to be buried alongside of her, but that was for you to decide.'

'We thought cremation was best,' he said.

'Yes, I know what folks say, but it doesn't seem decent to me. Still, I suppose burning him up is as good a way of getting rid of him as any. Nothing can bring him back now. All the same, if you don't mind, I'd rather stay home.'

So the two took their places in the car which stood behind the hearse and followed its slow progress through streets where children played, where women brushed their steps and men unloaded goods from parked vans. Noise swept against them and did not diminish or pause as they passed. A car overtook them, then held them up as it waited to turn. A bus stopped in front of them and its passengers stepped off and hurried between their two vehicles, looking into neither. He turned and regarded her and saw her face was set, her head held proudly as she looked out upon the incurious shoppers, upon impatient pedestrians waiting to cross the road, upon a man pulling out a striped sun blind above his shop window. Then as the brief cortège paused at traffic lights he saw her face change, the cheeks begin to work, and felt her hand slide up his thigh, seeking his.

And following where her eyes led, he saw standing by the pavement an old man, solitary, withered, his body shrunken in his clothes, his eyes faded and rheumy. Through thickening cataracts he peered into the hearse then stood back and held his body straight; and as they moved forward, he took the cap from his head and held it against his chest.

Other new fiction from Virago

L.C.
Susan Daitch

L.C. is an exceptional first novel. Inventive, daring and superbly constructed, it is a remarkable evocation of a nineteenth-century Frenchwoman's life as perceived by three very different women. At the heart of the book is the diary of L.C., Lucienne Crozier, in which she records an account of her arranged – and dull – marriage, her introduction to the Paris of art and politics, her affair with Romantic painter Eugène Delacroix, and her move towards a radical socialism and feminism in the tumultuous months before the 1848 revolution. After the uprising, Lucienne disappears without trace, her short life obliterated but for the testimony of her diary. When discovered some 120 years later, the task of translation is taken up first by Willa Rehnfield, a reclusive American with a predetermined view of the revolutionaries, and, after her death, by Jane Amme, a participant in the riots at Berkeley in 1968.

Three women of different ages, motivations, perspectives: each see in the diary her own version of truth. Susan Daitch has written an extraordinary novel which raises intriguing questions about the recording of history itself.

'A feminist novel in the best sense . . . Talented and extremely clever . . .a marvellous idea, beautifully expressed and worked out' – *Jane Miller*

Other new fiction from Virago

LEADEN WINGS
Zhang Jie
Translated by Gladys Yang

This wholly absorbing account of daily life in modern China is one of the first novels since the cultural revolution to be translated in the West. Central to its story is the Dawn Motor Works, symbol of Chinese industry. Ranged against the reformers who are trying to modernize it are all the forces of reaction, Chinese-style: the honest bewilderment of the old Party faithful, the political chicanery of those jockeying to stay in power. Zhang Jie highlights for us the lives of Autumn, the independent reporter; her adopted son Mo Zheng; Chen, the innovative manager; Zheng the crusading minister and many more. We glimpse a society where women reach high levels of power, yet still suffer from prejudices rooted in the feudal past: wives are subservient, widows pitied and divorcées condemned; girls should marry to please their parents; single women are eccentric, even sinister.

On its publication in China in 1980, *Leaden Wings* was both praised for its honesty and condemned for its satire. It has been described by one reviewer as 'China's first political novel'.

Zhang Jie, one of China's most controversial writers, was born in 1937 and worked for many years in industry. A writer since 1978, she lives in Peking. Gladys Yang, one of the most renowned Anglo-Chinese translators, also lives in Peking.